"Why Did You Run Out On Me?" He Asked.

"I have no intention of swimming through the muddy waters of the past," Molly said. "With your cynical judgment of me, I'd just be wasting my time anyway."

No doubt she was on the defensive and probably sounded as cynical as he did, but she didn't care. If she were going to survive this and keep her secret from him, she had to best him at his own game, or at least match him.

"What's wrong?" His eyes consumed her. "You look like something suddenly spooked you."

"I'm fine," she bit out.

"Liar."

"What do you want from me, Worth?"

"What if I said 'you'?"

Molly shook her head, trying to recover from the effect those words spoken in that sexy drawl had on her.

"I wouldn't believe you," she finally whispered.

Dear Reader,

What a pleasure to write the kind of books I love to read. What a pleasure to write, period. My career has evolved from teaching books, to selling books and now to writing books. I can't think of a career more rewarding or fun.

At the Texan's Pleasure is another tale in a list of many where there are secrets to hide. In this particular story the heroine is the one with the big secret. I love secrets. As I plot, it's so challenging and intriguing to figure out what my characters are hiding from each other—and oftentimes from themselves—then capitalize on those secrets.

I hope you, as my faithful reader, will feel the same way when you read *At the Texan's Pleasure*. Thank you for being so loyal and enjoying the written word, which, by the way, is one of my greatest passions.

Many happy endings!

Mary Lynn Baxter

MARY LYNN BAXTER

AT THE TEXAN'S PLEASURE

Silhouette® *Desire*

Published by Silhouette Books

America's Publisher of Contemporary Romance

SILHOUETTE BOOKS

ISBN-13: 978-0-373-76769-4
ISBN-10:   0-373-76769-2

AT THE TEXAN'S PLEASURE

Books by Mary Lynn Baxter

Silhouette Desire

Saddle Up #991
Tight-Fittin' Jeans #1057
Slow-Talkin' Texan #1177
Heart of Texas #1246
Her Perfect Man #1328
The Millionaire Comes Home #1387
Totally Texan #1713
To Claim His Own #1740
At the Texan's Pleasure #1769

MARY LYNN BAXTER

A native Texan, Mary Lynn Baxter knew instinctively that books would occupy an important part of her life. Always an avid reader, she became a school librarian, then a bookstore owner, before writing her first novel.

Now Mary Lynn Baxter is an award-winning author, who has written more than thirty novels, many of which have appeared on the *USA TODAY* list.

One

What was she doing?

Molly Stewart Bailey couldn't ignore her queasy stomach a moment longer, so she pulled off the highway onto the side of the road. Quickly she turned to see if her unexpected action had awakened her son Trent who was sound asleep in his car seat, his head lobbed to one side. For a second Molly considered jumping out of the car and propping his head back upright.

She squelched that idea as traffic was swishing by her at a rapid rate and in her present state of despair, she was liable to get run over. Still, she paused and continued to look at her son, who favored her, with dark brown hair, smoky blue eyes and clearly defined features.

A friend once told Molly she had the most uncluttered face ever. When she recalled that, it made her smile.

Not today.

Her mind was in too much turmoil; maybe that was why she kept her eyes on her child.

The only feature he had of his father was…

Suddenly Molly slammed the door shut on that thought. Now was the worst possible time to travel down memory lane. As it was, it would take every ounce of fortitude and courage she could muster to do what she was about to do. But she had no choice, even though choices had consequences. In this case, the consequences could change her life forever, and not for the better either.

That was why she had to guard her heart and its secret with every bit of fight she had in her.

Shaking her head to clear it, Molly pulled back onto the highway, soon to realize she was closer to the Cavanaugh Ranch than suspected. Once again she felt a wave of nausea wash through her. So much for her vow never to return to east Texas, much less to this precise location.

But then who could've known her mother would fall and injure her back to such an extent she was now bedridden? Molly stifled a sigh and tried to concentrate on something mundane like her surroundings, the tall oaks decorated in their fall colors of reds, browns and golds, the pines whose limbs seem to reach to the heavens—the ponds whose waters glistened like diamonds, and the meadowlands dotted with fenced-in cattle.

Only she found she couldn't fix her mind on anything other than gaining ground on her destination.

Nothing could usurp the fact that after almost five years she was about to see Worth Cavanaugh again. In the flesh. Cold chills darted through Molly, and she shivered. Stop it! she told herself. She had to get control of her splattered emotions and never let go of them. Otherwise, she was in for a world of hurt for the next couple of weeks, if not longer.

Gripping the steering wheel harder, Molly made the last turn before entering the long strip of graveled road which led to the ranch house atop the hill. Once there, she stopped the car and took several deep breaths, which helped settle her nerves. She'd known this endeavor wouldn't be easy, but she hadn't envisioned it being this difficult. It seemed that every nerve in her body was riding on the surface of her skin.

Not a good thing, she told herself, and not at all like her. As a registered nurse, she prided herself on having nerves of steel. Her job actually demanded it. But the *who* she was about to encounter didn't have anything to do with her job. It was personal. She would soon come face-to-face with the one man she had hoped never to see again, the man who had not only broken her heart but had jerked it out and stomped on it.

"Don't, Molly!" she chastised herself out loud, then quickly glanced in the rearview mirror at Trent. Her self-imposed rebuke hadn't impacted him at all. He was still sleeping soundly. She frowned, realizing that in a few moments, she'd have to awaken him, which would not be to his liking, or hers. When he didn't get his full nap, he tended to be grumpy and oftentimes hard to manage.

Waking up in a ranch setting would most likely right his world quickly, as she'd been telling him about the horses and cattle he'd see every day. She had even bought him a new pair of cowboy boots and hat in honor of this visit to see his grandmother.

Trent had insisted on wearing his new attire today, which brought a smile to Molly's face, recalling how he'd paraded around the house, peering at himself in the mirror every chance he got, a big grin on his face.

Another sigh filtered through her at the same time the smile disappeared. Worth's house stood in front of her, and for a second she was tempted to jerk the gearshift in Reverse and back down the drive. Out of sight; out of mind. That thought was only fleeting as the needy edge in her mother's voice rose up to haunt her, recalling this visit wasn't about her, Molly, but rather her mother.

As long as she kept that uppermost in her mind, she would do just fine. Molly owed Maxine Stewart more than she could ever hope to repay, and not because she was her mother, either. Maxine had stood by her, though she had been kept in the dark about much of what had gone on in her daughter's life these last few years. If for no other reason, Molly would always love her for that.

"Mommy."

Glad for the interruption, Molly flung her head around and smiled at her son who was now wide-eyed and kicking his booted feet. "Hey, it's about time you woke up."

"When can I see the horses and cows?" Trent asked right off the bat.

Molly grinned. "First things first, okay? We'll see Granna, then the animals."

"Granna'll take me."

Molly heard that comment just as she exited the Toyota Camry and came around to release Trent from his car seat. Then helping him out, she said, "Remember Granna can't do anything. She's in bed with a hurt back."

Trent frowned as he jumped to the ground, his eyes scanning the surroundings. Molly followed suit, taking in the lovely manicured lawn close to the modern ranch house. Then her gaze dipped beyond to the sloping grounds where animals grazed in the distance near a blue pond.

"Mommy, look, I see lots of cows."

"Me, too," Molly said absently, turning Trent by the shoulders and steering him in the direction of the side door to her mother's small living quarters. Although Maxine's bedroom and sitting room were part of the main house, Worth had been thoughtful enough to add a private entrance, for which Molly was especially grateful today.

As splintered as she was, she didn't need to run into Worth, not until she'd at least seen her mother and found out for herself how seriously she was injured. Beyond that, Molly intended to take the moments as they came and deal with them no matter how painful or unsettling.

"Mom, we're here," Molly called out, knocking on the door, then opening it.

Maxine Stewart lay propped up on a pillow in her bed, a broad smile on her still-attractive face, her arms reaching out to Trent, who seemed hesitant to move.

"It's okay, honey, go give Granna a hug."

"I'm expecting a big hug, you cutie tootie. Granna's been waiting a long time for this day."

Though Trent still appeared reluctant, he made his way toward his grandmother and let her put her arms around him, giving him a bear hug. Finally pushing Trent to arm's length, Maxine's eyes glistened with tears. "My, what a big boy you are."

"I'll be five my next birthday," Trent said with pride.

Maxine winked at him. "Granna hasn't forgotten. I already have your birthday present."

"Wow!" Trent said with awe.

"Don't get too excited," Molly cautioned. "Next month you'll only be four and a half, which means your birthday's a while off yet."

"Can I have it now?"

Molly grinned, tousling his hair. "Not a chance, boy." Then it was her turn to hug her mother, though through it all, her heart took yet another beating, but for an entirely different reason.

Maxine's once unlined face had wrinkles that were unavoidably noticeable and dark circles under her eyes where none used to be. Her mother appeared frail, so much frailer than she had ever been.

Though Maxine wasn't a robust woman, she'd always been the picture of health and beauty. Friends and strangers who saw the two of them together knew they were mother and daughter because they favored each other so much. Some even told them they could pass for sisters.

Pain. That was the culprit that had so changed and aged her mother. Peering at Maxine closely through trained eyes, Molly didn't see any signs of that pain turning Maxine loose any time soon, not if the X-rays her doctor had sent Molly to peruse were correct. At this point, Molly saw no reason to question the diagnosis.

"Mom, how are you really doing?" Molly asked into the short silence.

"Good."

Molly rolled her eyes. "Hey, remember who you're talking to."

Maxine made a face. "A nurse, I know."

"All the more reason you need to be honest and 'fess up."

"Okay, my back hurts like you-know-what," Maxine admitted down in the mouth, casting a glance at Trent who was busy wandering around the room, fingering this and that.

"That's why I'm here."

"Only not for long, surely." Maxine made a face. "You just can't leave your job. I'd feel even worse if you lost it because of me."

"Hey, calm down," Molly said, leaning down and kissing Maxine on the cheek. "I have a great doctor for a boss. Besides, I have sick days, as well as vacation days, I haven't used. Four weeks' worth, actually."

"Still…"

"It's all right, I promise. I'm not going to do anything that puts my career in jeopardy."

Maxine gave a visible sigh of relief. "I'm glad to hear that." She smiled. "It's so good to see you and Trent. You're a sight for my sore eyes." Maxine faced her grandson and her smile widened. "He's grown so much since I last saw him."

"He's growing much too fast," Molly said with a crack in her voice. "He's no longer my baby."

"That's not so." Maxine looked back at Molly. "He'll always be your baby just like you'll always be mine."

Tears welled up in Molly's eyes, but she blinked them away, hopefully before her mother could see them. "So tell me what's going on here."

"Are you referring to my job?"

Molly was taken aback. "No. I wouldn't think there's a problem with that."

"I hope you're right," Maxine said, her brows drawing together. "Worth let me hire a part-time helper several months ago, which is good. She's more or less running the house now, with me telling her what to do, of course."

"So is that working out?"

"Yes, but this home needs a full-time housekeeper, especially with Worth thinking about entering politics."

The last person Molly wanted to talk about was Worth. Actually, she'd rather not know anything about him *period*. Under the circumstances, she knew that wasn't possible.

"I just can't help but be a little fearful of eventually losing my job," Maxine said, "especially if I don't start improving."

"Oh, come on, Mom, Worth's not going to let you go. You know better than that."

"Maybe I do, but you know how your mind plays tricks on you and convinces you otherwise." Maxine paused. "I guess what I'm saying is that my mind is my own worst enemy."

"That comes from lying in bed with nothing to keep you occupied." Molly smiled with a wink. "But now that Trent and I are here, that's going to change." Speaking of Trent made her turn to check on him, only to find he was no longer in the room.

"Did you see Trent leave?" Molly asked, trying to temper her building panic.

"No, but he can't go far."

That was when she noticed the door leading to the main house was open. "I'll be right back," Molly flung over her shoulder as she dashed out of the room, soon finding herself in the house's main living area. "Trent Bailey, where are you?"

"Who is Trent?"

Molly stopped in her tracks, and stared into the face of Worth Cavanaugh. For what seemed the longest time, not only did her body shut down, but their eyes also met and locked, though neither said a word. But that didn't matter. The tension was such that they might as well have been screaming at one another.

"Hello, Worth." Somehow Molly managed to get those words through cotton-dry lips.

"What are you doing here?" he demanded in a curt tone, choosing to ignore her greeting.

"I would think that's obvious."

"Maxine failed to tell me you were coming." Instead of curt, his tone was now in the freezer, showing no chance of thawing.

"That's also obvious."

Another silence.

"Again, who's Trent?"

"My son."

Worth's black eyes flickered and his mouth stretched into a

pencil-thin line. "Lucky you," he finally said in a caustic tone, his eyes filled with scorn as they traveled up and down her body.

The word *bastard* was about to fly out of her mouth when Trent rounded the corner, racing to her side. "Mommy, I went to see the moo cows."

Molly pulled him against her, clamping her hand on his shoulder. When he started to squirm, her hold tightened. As if sensing he was in trouble, Trent stopped wiggling and stared up at Worth with open curiosity.

"Trent," Molly said in a tight voice, "this is Mr. Cavanaugh."

Worth merely nodded at the boy, then looking up at Molly said, "I'd like to talk to you alone."

Biting back another choice word, Molly peered down at Trent. "Go back to Granna's room, honey. And don't leave. I'll be there shortly."

"Okay," Trent said, whirling and running back down the hall.

Don't run, Molly wanted to shout, but she knew it wouldn't do any good. Trent was already out of hearing range.

"So how old is he?"

Molly shook her head as though to clear it, Worth's question taking her by surprise. "Almost four," she said, lying with such ease that it shocked her.

"Good-looking kid."

"Thanks."

Instead of receding, the tension between them continued to rise until Molly felt either she or the room would explode. Or maybe both. She sensed Worth felt the same way, as his features seemed to darken by the second.

"How long are you planning to stay?" he asked, the muscle in one jaw moving up and down, something that always happened when he was angry or disturbed.

"I'm not sure." She paused. "Maybe a week. Maybe longer. I'm not sure. Do you have a problem with my being here?"

"Not in the least," he countered in a harsh tone.

"Is there an addendum to that?"

"Yeah," he said in a parting shot, "just stay out of *my* way."

Two

He'd been blindsided and he hated it.

This was *his* domain, dammit, and he had control over what went on here. Or at least he thought he did. Worth muttered a curse, rubbing the five o'clock shadow that covered a good portion of his face as he continued to stand on the porch outside his room. In the distance, he could see the last remnants of a sun fast sinking into oblivion.

Worth peered at his watch and noted that it was not quite five. He loved the fall of the year, especially October because the leaves changed colors. There was one exception, however. The time change. He didn't like anything about falling backward, robbing him of an hour of light at the end of day. As a hands-on rancher, light was a precious commodity.

At this particular moment, whether it was daylight or not wasn't what his frustration was all about. Time had nothing to do with the gnawing deep in his gut. But he sure as hell knew what did.

Molly.

Back in his life.

No way.

Not possible.

Not happening.

Only it had.

She was in his house.

And there wasn't one thing he could do about it short of pitching her and the kid out the door. He muttered another colorful expletive, but again that did nothing to untie the growing knot in his stomach.

Granted, he'd known he would eventually see her again. To think not would've been ludicrous and unrealistic. After all, her mother worked for him. But since he hadn't seen Molly in nearly five years, he'd begun to think that maybe fate was smiling on him.

Heretofore, during her vacation, Maxine had always gone to visit Molly. He'd assumed that would continue to be the case.

Of course, that was before Maxine had fallen and injured her back to the extent she'd been confined to bed. Molly returning to the ranch seemed to fit the logical order of events, which wouldn't have been as much of a problem, if only he'd known about it.

He didn't like surprises, especially not surprises of this nature. Almost walking head-on into her had definitely been a blow—a blow from which he hadn't yet recovered.

The kid hadn't helped, either.

Worth rubbed the back of his neck, feeling the hard coiled muscles under his fingers. Nothing short of asking them to leave would give him any relief. That wasn't about to happen, at least not for several days anyway.

Meanwhile, he'd just have to put up with the situation. If Molly did like she was told and stayed out of his way, then he could manage. If not… Hell, he wasn't about to go down that treacherous road. It would only make him madder and more frustrated.

He just wished she still didn't look so damn good. Lovelier than even he remembered. And his memory was excellent. Never a day went by that some little something didn't remind him of her. While that never failed to shoot his blood pressure up, he'd learned to shove thoughts of her aside and move on.

Now though, that wasn't doable. He'd most likely see her every day whether he wanted to or not, regardless of what he'd told her. Having gotten over the initial shock somewhat and his head screwed back on straight had brought that reality home. As long as she was on his property, he couldn't avoid her altogether. He couldn't avoid the kid, either.

No doubt about it, she couldn't deny the kid. Looked just like her, which wasn't a bad thing. Molly's dark hair that reminded him of soot, was short and stylish, a perfect backdrop for those smoky colored eyes. And that sultry voice—God, it had always been a turn-on and still was.

Even though he knew she was twenty-seven, seven years younger than he, she didn't look it. With her unmarked skin that reminded him of porcelain at its finest, she could pass for less than twenty.

However, if one were to look closer, her figure bore testimony to her actual age. While remaining thin, with a to-die-for body, he noticed that it was more rounded, even slightly voluptuous in certain places, particularly her breasts and stomach.

Having borne a child was responsible for those added factors. Instead of detracting from her beauty, they merely enhanced it, making her body sexier than ever. Though he was loathe to admit it, he'd have to be dead not to notice. He might be many things, but dead wasn't one of them.

There had been times, however, when he'd wished he were dead. All because of her.

After Molly had run off, leaving him high and dry, she'd killed something vital inside him, which had never been revived. Part of his heart and soul were dead and Molly was to blame.

He despised her for that.

At least that was what he'd always told himself. But seeing her for that few minutes had turned his perfect world upside down—socked him in the gut, actually. Only not for long, he vowed. Already he was remembering her for the liar she really was.

And with that recall, his confidence rebounded. Even though she was staying in a small suite not far from his didn't mean one damn thing, although at first he'd questioned his placement of her and Trent.

Then he'd told himself, what the hell. Where she stayed didn't mean a thing to him. Hence, he'd had Maxine's part-time helper, Kathy, show them to that particular suite, mainly because it was close to Molly's mother.

In addition, he'd reminded himself, she wouldn't be at the ranch long enough to matter where she slept. He knew she was a nurse with some large doctors' group in Houston. Hell, he'd heard Maxine brag about that until she'd finally gotten the message that he wasn't interested in hearing about her daughter.

He often wondered what Molly had told her mother about their past relationship. He suspected it had been nowhere near the truth, which reinforced his anger. A good thing, he told himself. As long as he held onto that anger and hatred, he'd come out the winner.

And to hell with her.

Suddenly Worth heard a phone ring. It was only after the third ring he realized it was his cell. Without checking who was calling, he barked, "Cavanaugh."

"My, you sound like you're in a sour mood."

"Hello, Olivia."

He didn't miss the aggravated sigh that filtered through the line. "Is that all you have to say?"

"What do you want me to say?"

"Hello, sweetheart, would do for starters."

He didn't answer. First, he'd never called her sweetheart and didn't intend to start now. Second, but most important, she'd hit the nail on the head. He was in a sour mood, but now was not the time to tell her why. He simply wasn't up to fighting the war that would occur if he told her Molly was back in town, staying at the ranch.

More to the point, it wasn't any of Olivia's business.

"Okay, you win," Olivia replied in an offhanded manner. "I'll let you pout, or whatever the hell you're doing."

"Did you want anything in particular?" Worth asked in a cold tone, knowing he was being a first-class jerk. Yet he felt no need to apologize.

"What time are you picking me up?"

Worth's mind went blank. "Picking you up?"

"Yes," she said, not bothering to hide her growing irritation. "Remember you promised to take me to dinner tonight."

"Oh, right."

"You'd forgotten all about that, hadn't you?"

He had, but again he wasn't going to admit it. "I'll be there around sevenish."

Another sigh. "You know, Worth, I think you take great pride in being an ass."

Silence.

"And while we're on the subject of dinner," Olivia added,

"don't forget about the party at my house tomorrow night concerning your political future."

"I haven't, Olivia." His tone was weary. "I know my parents are invited along with a possible potential backer."

"At least you remembered something."

With that, she hung up.

That was two women he'd ruffled today. He wondered if his mother was next in line. Probably so, he told himself. On a normal day, he and Eva Cavanaugh didn't see eye-to-eye on much of anything. If she'd stop trying to micromanage his life, that might change. His father, however, was a different matter. They got along fine, at least on the surface, though he felt he had never known what made Ted Cavanaugh tick.

In all fairness, his parents probably didn't know what made him tick, either. One thing he did know was they wanted him to marry Olivia Blackburn. No. They *expected* him to marry her, which was the same as waving a red flag in front of a bull. He didn't live by, or under, others' expectations. Besides, he didn't love Olivia. He'd made the mistake of falling in love once, and he'd never repeat it. Never.

Only problem was, he needed what Olivia could give him and that land she stood to inherit. His parents had deeded him the three hundred acres that adjoined their property, which he'd hoped would be enough to do most anything he chose in the way of ranching. But with his cattle business thriving, he needed more land.

That was where Olivia fit into his life so well. The acreage she'd inherit from her father would give him the room to expand his horse breeding business, a dream that hadn't yet come to fruition.

Ah, to hell with women and the garbage they dished out, his thoughts targeting Molly. What he needed was a drink, he told himself savagely. Something large and strong that would cut through the constriction in his throat that had a stranglehold on him.

He was just about to accommodate himself when his phone rang again. This time he did look at caller ID and saw that it was his mother. He was tempted not to answer it, but he did. Maybe she was canceling the dinner. A smirk crossed his lips. Not a chance that would happen.

"Yo, Mother."

"Is that any way for a politician to answer the phone?"

"I'm not a politician. Yet." He was irritated and it showed.

"You will be," she said in her lofty tone. "Just as soon as you throw your hat into the ring."

"I haven't decided to do that, either."

"I don't know why you take delight in being difficult."

"Mother, if you're going to get on your soapbox about politics, then this conversation is over."

"Don't you dare hang up on me."

Not only could he hear the chagrin in his mother's voice, but he could picture it in her face, as well. Although tall and rawboned like himself, she was nonetheless a very striking woman, with blond hair and black eyes, who commanded attention with her height and flare for fashion. But when she was out of sorts, which she was now, her usually pleasant features turned hard and unpleasant.

"I'll see you and Dad tomorrow night at Liv's around eight. We can talk about politics then, okay?"

"That's not what I'm calling about."

Something in her voice alerted him to be on guard, that the rest of the conversation would not be to his liking. Her next words confirmed that.

"Why didn't you tell me?"

"Tell you what?" Worth's tone was as innocent as hers was accusing.

"That Molly Bailey, or whatever her name is now, is at your ranch."

God, it didn't take long for news to travel, but then in a small town like Sky, Texas gossip was the most popular game in town.

"Because it's no big deal."

"No big deal." Eva's voice rose. "How can you say that?"

"Because it's true. She came to see about her mother."

"I understand that."

"So what's the problem?"

"The fact that she's staying at your place is the problem."

"Mother, I don't want to discuss this."

Eva went on as though he hadn't said a word. "A motel would've been just fine for the likes of her."

Although he had no intention of defending Molly—not for one second—his mother's words set him off like a rocket. It was all he could do to keep his cool long enough to get off the phone before he said something he'd be sorry for.

"Goodbye, Mother. I'll see you tomorrow tonight."

"Worth Cavanaugh, you can't hang—"

"Yes, I can. I've got to go now." Without further ado, Worth punched the red button on the phone and Eva's hostile voice was no longer assaulting his ear.

Women!

He'd had enough of them for one day. That stiff drink was looking more enticing by the second. He was about to walk back inside when he saw her strolling across the lawn. Alone.

Worth stopped in his tracks and watched. Molly was still dressed in the same jeans she'd had on earlier, jeans that fit her rear to perfection. Right now, it was her backside that held him captive—the sway of those perfect hips. Then she turned slightly, giving him privy to the way her full breasts jutted against the soft forest-green sweater.

For what seemed an eternity, his eyes consumed her. Then

muttering a harsh obscenity, he felt his manhood rise to the occasion. Even though he dragged his gaze away from the provocative thrust of those breasts and back to her face, that action did nothing to release the pressure behind his zipper.

She was such an awesome picture of beauty against the gold and orange leaves falling from the trees that his breath caught in his throat.

It was in that moment she looked up and saw him. For the second time in a day, their eyes met and held.

He stared at her, breathing hard. Then cursing again for the fool that he was, Worth pivoted on a booted heel and strode back inside, only to realize that he was shaking all over.

Three

Lucky for her it was Worth who looked away first. For some crazy reason, Molly couldn't seem to tear her eyes away from him, although he was several yards from her. Yet his tall figure appeared clear to her.

And threatening.

Even so, she had been held spellbound by his presence, though she knew that if she were close enough to read those black eyes, they would be filled with animosity.

Thank heaven the moment had passed and he was gone. However, she didn't move. Her body felt disassembled, perhaps like one of the many leaves that were falling from the trees, never to be attached again.

What an insane thought, Molly told herself brutally, storming back into her room. Besides, it was getting downright chilly despite the fact the sun was still hanging on. Once it disappeared, the temperature had a tendency to drop quickly.

By the time she closed the French doors, she was shivering all over. Not from the chill, she knew, but from her second encounter with Worth. She eased onto the chaise longue, the closest seat, and took several deep breaths to calm her racing heart, feeling lucky to be alone. Trent was with his grandmother who was happy as a lark reading to him. He had crawled into the bed with Maxine and was hanging onto every word she read out of the book.

Before she had ventured outdoors, Molly had stood in her mother's door and watched them, feeling a peace descend over her. Coming here, despite the obstacles, had been the right thing to do. Not only did her ailing mother need her daughter, she needed to get to really know her grandson. To date, Trent and Maxine hadn't had the opportunity to bond, to develop a close relationship that was so unique to grandparents and grandchildren.

Now, however, the doubts were once again creeping back into her mind, following that long distance encounter with Worth. Molly bit down on her lower lip to stop it from trembling while her eyes perused the room where she tried hard to concentrate on the rustic good taste that surrounded her.

She forced herself to take in, and appreciate, the cobalt blue walls and the big four-poster bed that was angled in one corner. The one thing that held her attention was the handmade quilt that adorned the bed. The coverlet picked up the blue in the wall, as well as other vivid colors, resulting in a stunning piece of art.

An armoire occupied the other side of the bedroom. The sitting area where the chaise resided held a desk and chair. No doubt, it was a place where she could be comfortable for a long period of time. But even if her job allowed that luxury, it wouldn't work.

Because of Worth.

Suddenly Molly felt tears fill her eyes, and that made her mad. Lunging off the chaise, she curled her fists into her palms and strengthened her resolve. She wouldn't let her emotions get the best of her again. She had indulged herself before she'd arrived, and that had to be her swan song. Otherwise, she wouldn't get through the quagmire that was already threatening to suck her under.

Yet seeing Worth again so soon after her arrival seemed to have imprinted him on her brain, and she couldn't let go of that image. What an image it was, too. She had never thought of him as handsome, only sexy.

Now he seemed both. He was tall and leathery thin, but not too thin, having toned his muscles to perfection riding horses and branding cattle—the two loves of his life. His short brown hair still had streaks of blond, but she could almost swear that some gray had been added to the mix. His face, with its chiseled features, was definitely more lined.

Neither change, however, was a detraction because of those incredible black eyes, surrounded by equally incredible thick lashes. They were by far the focal point of his face and his best asset.

And he knew how to use them. He had a way of looking at her like she was the only one in existence. And that was a real turn-on, or at least it always had been for her.

Until today.

When she had practically run into him upon her arrival, she'd seen none of that sexual charisma reflected in his eyes. Instead, she'd seen pure hostility and anger that bordered on hatred. Another shiver darted through Molly, and she crossed her arms over her chest as if to protect herself.

From Worth?

Possibly, because he was someone she no longer knew. More noticeable than the physical changes in him, were the changes in attitude. From the first moment she'd met him that fateful summer, she remembered him as having been rather cocky and self-assured for someone who was just twenty-nine years old. But she'd taken no offense at that attitude; actually that was one of the reasons she'd been attracted to him.

While both cocky and self-assured still applied, other adjectives now fit his personality. He appeared bitter, cynical and completely unbending. Though she didn't know the reason for such a radical change, she didn't like it, especially since it was directed at her.

After all, *he'd* been the one who had betrayed her. If anyone had an ax to grind, it was she. Admittedly she did, but she wasn't about to show her bitterness to the entire world.

Maybe she was just the one who continually brought out the worst in him. Around others maybe he was a kinder and gentler soul. That thought almost brought a smile to Molly's face. Worth Cavanaugh was a man *unto* himself, having carved an empire *for* himself in his early thirties. Kinder and gentler didn't make that happen. Hard and tough-skinned did.

Suddenly a sliver of panic ran down Molly's spine. What was she doing here? It wasn't going to work. She hadn't even been here one whole day, and thoughts of Worth had her by the jugular and wouldn't let go.

Molly swallowed convulsively as she eased back onto the chaise, vivid memories of the last time they were together rising to haunt her. If her recall served her correctly, she'd been in the barn that day, looking for Worth most likely.

The why actually hadn't been important. Once there, she'd climbed into the loft and plopped down in the middle of the hay. She remembered closing her eyes, taking a catnap during which she dreamed about Worth. When she finally opened her eyes, she was taken aback to find him leaning against a post, watching her with unsuppressed desire further darkening his eyes.

Since it had been summer and the temperature sizzling, she'd had on only the barest of clothing—a pair of blue jean shorts, a tank top without a bra and flip-flops. The way he'd stared at her, she might as well have been naked.

Heat pooled between her thighs as their eyes remained locked.

She saw him swallow with effort, causing his Adam's apple to bob up and down as he slowly, but surely pushed away from the post and made his way toward her, his fingers busily unzipping his jeans.

All of that seemed to take place in slow motion as she lay unmoving, her heart pumping so loudly she could hear it in her ears. By the time he reached her, Molly's eyes were no longer on his face but rather on the juncture at his thighs where his erection was thick and hard.

She couldn't speak; her mouth was too dry. She could only watch him lift his arms and pull off his T-shirt, then toss it aside. A gasp slipped past her lips as her eyes covered every inch of his big, beautiful body, settling on his erection that seemed to be increasing by the moment.

Blood pounded from her heart into her head at such a rapid rate that it made her dizzy. Yet she couldn't have removed her eyes from him if someone had threatened her life with a gun. It wasn't as if that had been the first time she'd seen him in the buff, either.

It hadn't. Far from it, actually.

Since her arrival that summer at his ranch, she and Worth had become an instant item. It had been lust at first sight.

When that lust had turned to love, Molly couldn't say. Maybe it had been after he'd taken her that first time. From then on, he hadn't been able to keep his hands off her and vice versa. With summer coming to an end, nothing had changed. Every time Worth looked at her, or came near her, her bones melted.

That day was no exception.

"You're a beautiful man," she said in her sultry voice that now had a crack in it.

He merely grinned, then knelt beside her and promptly removed her clothing.

"Not nearly as beautiful as you," he rasped, his gaze now covering every inch of her flesh.

He bent over and latched onto an already burgeoning nipple and sucked it until she couldn't keep still. Finally releasing it, he moved to the other one and did likewise. Only after he left her breasts and began to lick his way down her stomach did she take action, latching onto his erection, rubbing her thumb in and around the opening.

Worth let out a loud groan as he nudged her legs apart and gently inserted two fingers inside her.

"Oh, yes," she whimpered, her hips going crazy.

"Baby, baby, you're so wet, so ready."

"Please, now. Don't make me wait."

Propping himself on his hands, Worth leaned further over her, then entered her with unerring accuracy. For a moment he didn't move, seemingly to enjoy the way she formed a tight sheath around him, his eyes burning deeply into hers.

Then he pumped up and down until the fiery explosion hit them at the same time. Moments later he lay limp on her with her arms clasped tightly around him.

"Am I too heavy?" he whispered at last, his breath caressing her ear.

"No."

"Oh, but I am." He chuckled, then rolled over so that she was now on top of him.

She leaned down, kissed him, and said in an awed voice, "I can't believe you're still inside me."

"Me, either, especially since all the lead's gone out of my pencil."

She giggled and kissed him again.

Suddenly his gaze darkened on her. "Know what?"

"I know lots of whats," she said in a teasing voice. "One of them is that I love you."

"I love you, too, so much that I got carried away and didn't use a condom."

For several seconds, silence fell between them.

"Are you mad at me?" he asked.

"No," Molly responded, feeling her brows gather in a frown. "It takes two to tango, as the saying goes."

"Right, but I should've been more responsible."

"Shh. It's okay. It's not the right time of the month for me." Molly paused. "At least I don't think so."

"I'm sorry."

"Don't you dare say that. I loved every minute of it. There's nothing to be sorry about."

It was the thought of those words that jerked Molly out of the past back into the present. *Back to reality.* To the pain and hurt that had resulted from that passionate afternoon of lovemaking.

Knowing her face was drenched with tears, Molly went into the bathroom and wet a washcloth with cold water. Though the cloth felt like ice against her skin, it did what she'd hoped it would and that was clear her fogged mind.

She couldn't change what had happened between her and Worth. All she could do was change how she reacted to him now. Though the aftermath of their affair had left deep and lasting scars, she wasn't sorry because out of it had come the blessing of her life—her son.

For that she would never be sorry.

It was then that Molly suddenly heard the sound of an engine. Hurrying to the French doors, she walked onto the porch where she saw Worth sitting in his truck. She was still standing in the cold when the taillights disappeared.

With her teeth chattering, she went back inside, not stopping until she was in her mother's room, facing her son's animated face.

"Mommy, Mommy, come see what Granna gave me."

Squaring her shoulders, Molly shoved the past back under lock and key deep in her soul.

Four

"Oh, Doctor, thanks so much for returning my call."

"Not a problem," Dr. Roy Coleman responded. "I know you're concerned about your mother and well you should be."

Molly winced under the doctor's direct words, but then she was a nurse, for God's sake, so she shouldn't be surprised. Most doctors nowadays didn't tiptoe around the rose bush. They called the problem as they saw it and let the chips fall where they may. Her boss Sam Nutting was cut from that same bolt of cloth.

Somehow, though, she was reluctant to hear the truth because it was her mother, who had always been Molly's lifeline and still was. Her dad had died from heart failure when she was young, leaving them without ample resources. Hence, Maxine had had to work her fingers to the bone for other people in order for them to survive. However, she never forsook her daughter; Maxine always found time to spend with Molly no matter how exhausted she was, or how much she had to do.

"Are you still there, Ms. Bailey?"

The doctor's crisp voice brought Molly back to the moment at hand. "Sorry, I was woolgathering about Mother, actually. Now that I've seen her and the condition she's in, I'm really concerned."

"As I said earlier, you have good reason. She took a nasty fall, which did major damage to her back, as you already know, of course. The main plus, however, is that she has no fractures."

Even though Maxine had slipped in the hallway two weeks ago, it seemed much longer to Molly because she hadn't been able to leave work and come immediately. Her mother had insisted that she not, making light of the accident.

Only after Dr. Coleman talked with her, then sent copies of the MRI did Molly know the extent of the damage to her mother's back. Ergo, she lost no time in rushing to Maxine's side.

"I appreciate you keeping me posted at every turn, Doctor."

"Wouldn't have it any other way. As I told you, Maxine's special, a rare breed. I know she's in pain, yet she suffers in silence."

"Only that's not good."

"You're right. It's not. I don't want her in pain. But Maxine is one of—if not the most—hardheaded patients I have."

"That's why I'm here, Dr. Coleman, to see that she does like she's told and behaves herself."

He chuckled, and Molly liked that. Although she'd never met him, they'd had countless phone conversations. Each time she was more impressed with his sense of humor and his care of her mother.

"I'd like to get another MRI soon, so we can see if the severely strained muscles are beginning to heal on their own.

Meanwhile, I've ordered a corset for her to wear. In fact, I don't want her even sitting on the side of the bed without it, much less walking."

Molly tried to remain upbeat, but under the circumstances that was becoming more difficult by the second. "That sounds like she's going to be incapacitated for a good little while."

"Because of her osteoporosis, she will be."

Molly's heart sank. "So we're looking at long-term recovery instead of short-term." A flat statement of fact.

"Not necessarily. Maxine is so determined that she could rebound much quicker than most, I suspect." Dr. Coleman paused. "However, work of any kind is out for now."

"What about physical therapy?"

"That's coming, but it's too soon. The corset is enough for now."

Molly fought back the unknown fears that were festering inside her. For the moment, the picture was dismal. What if her mother never regained the full use of her body? Maxine had always worked, had always been full of energy. She didn't believe in resting on her laurels, she'd told that to Molly all her life. An honest day's work for an honest day's pay had been Maxine's philosophy.

"You're going to have to help me convince *her* that she can't work, Doctor. So far I don't think you've gotten that across to her. She thinks she'll be mopping floors next week."

"Someone will be mopping floors, but it won't be Maxine."

"Thank you for being brutally honest with me." Molly's sigh was shaky. "Now, I have to be brutally honest with her."

"If you want to wait, I'll drive out to the ranch. We'll gang up on her."

A doctor who made house calls? No way. Yet he had offered, though Molly wasn't about to take him up on that offer. She could handle Maxine, but it wouldn't be easy. No matter. Her mother had no choice but to comply.

"Thank you for your kindness, but let me have a go at it first. If she bucks me, you'll be the first to know."

"Call me any time."

When the conversation ended, Molly held the receiver for a few moments longer, then replaced it, feeling as though she was moving in a daze.

She had dreaded having this session with the doctor because she knew it wasn't going to be encouraging. Since her arrival yesterday, she had come to realize her mother was indeed in dire straits, with no easy fix.

Now this morning, she had the unpleasant task of breaking the bad news to her mother. Molly was just thankful Trent was with Maxine. Bless his sweet heart, he had rarely left Maxine's room since they had arrived, seeming to have forgotten the horses and cattle with which he'd been so fascinated. But then Maxine had played with him non-stop. Knowing Maxine was exhausted, Molly finally had to call a halt to their togetherness.

Putting off the inevitable wasn't going to make things any easier, Molly reminded herself. Squaring her shoulders with resolve, she left her room and headed toward Maxine's, though not without first taking a furtive look around. While she certainly didn't expect Worth to be lurking in the shadows waiting to pounce on her, she still found herself somewhat rattled every time she left her room.

She had no idea what time Worth returned home last night, but she knew it was late, having heard him open the door to his room. It didn't matter where he went or what he did. Their relationship was past history and she had no right or reason to care about his whereabouts. Her aim was to avoid him at all costs.

Only problem with that, she was staying under his roof.

Pushing that unsettling thought aside, Molly knocked lightly on Maxine's door, then went in, only to pull up short. Her mother was asleep while Trent lay sprawled beside her, coloring in his coloring book.

"Hi, Mommy," he said in a soft voice. "Granna felled asleep."

"It's okay, honey." She reached for him and lifted him off the bed, then gathered the books and colors. "I want you to go to our room and color there for a few minutes, okay?"

Trent made a face. "I don't want to."

She smiled. "I know, but again, it'll only be for a few minutes, then I'll come and get you. I want to talk to Granna alone."

"Why can't I stay?" he whined.

Molly gave him a stern look. "Trent."

With his bottom lip poked out, he took the stuff, and without further ado, made his way to the door.

"Don't go anywhere else. Stay put in our room."

"Okay," he mumbled.

Molly stood watch until he was down the hall and the door closed behind him. He was so precious. Rarely did she ever have to scold him, but she didn't want him to hear this conversation she was about to have with her mother. She feared Maxine's reaction would not be favorable.

"Mom," Molly said, gently touching Maxine on the shoulder.

Her mother's eyes popped open and for a moment, she seemed completely disoriented. Then when she apparently recognized Molly, she smiled in relief, only then to frown. "Where's Trent?"

"He's in our room. He'll be back shortly."

"What time is it?" Maxine asked, her frown deepening.

"Almost noon."

"Oh, dear. I can't believe I even went to sleep, much less for that long."

"It's okay, Mother. You need all the rest you can get."

"No, what I need is to spend time with my daughter and grandson before I go back to work."

Molly was quiet for a moment, her mind scrabbling for a way to tell her mother the truth without breaking her heart. "Mom—"

"You're going to tell me I can't go back to work any time soon, aren't you?" Maxine's eyes were keen on Molly.

"That's right," Molly declared with relief.

"No, that's wrong."

Molly's relief was short-lived. "I—"

"I'm going to be just fine. I know I pulled some muscles in my back—"

"That you did," Molly interrupted flatly. "And according to the doctor, your recovery won't be quick or easy."

Maxine's chin began to wobble. "I refuse to believe that."

"It's the truth, Mother, and you have to face it. More than that, you have to accept it. Now if you didn't already have osteoporosis, then maybe things would be different."

"But what about my job?" Maxine wailed. "Worth has been so good to me, but he'll hire someone permanently to take my place. He'll have to, only I can't bear that thought."

"Mom, let's not beat that dead horse again. Worth is not going to replace you."

"Has he told you that?" Maxine's tone held a bit of belligerence.

Molly hesitated. "No, he hasn't."

"So you don't know what he has in mind." Maxine's voice broke.

"Oh, Mom, please, don't worry. It's going to be all right." Molly caressed one of Maxine's cheeks.

"He doesn't know—" Again Maxine broke off.

"The whole story about your back," Molly cut in. "Is that what you were about to say?"

Maxine merely nodded.

"Ah, so you told him what you wanted him to know, what you thought he wanted to hear."

Maxine reached for a tissue out of the nearby box. "I can't believe this is happening."

"Look, Mom, it's not as grim as you think."

"That's because it's not you." Maxine paused, then added quickly, "For which I'm grateful. I couldn't stand it if it were you in this shape."

"Yes, you could. You'd just come and take care of me like I'm going to do for you."

"You can't," Maxine wailed again. "You have a child and a job. And your life. You can't—"

"Shh," Molly said softly. "Enough. I'm not going to give up my life, for pity's sake. Just rest easy, I have a plan."

"What?" Maxine's tone was suspicious.

"I'll tell you later." Molly leaned over and kissed her mother on the cheek. "Right now, I'm going to send Trent back in here unless you want to go back to sleep."

"Not on your life. I want to spend every moment I can with my grandson."

"By the way, I spoke to Dr. Coleman."

Maxine's chin wobbled again.

"Hey, stop it. I'll tell you about that later also. Meanwhile, keep your chin up, you hear? Everything's going to work out."

Maxine did her best to smile. "Send my boy back to me. I have plans that don't include you."

Molly smiled big, then sobered. "Don't let him wear you out. He can, you know."

"You let me worry about that."

When Molly reached her room, she realized tears were running down her face. Brushing them aside, she forced a smile and opened the door. "Hey, kiddo, Granna's waiting on you."

* * *

Would there ever come a time when she wouldn't react to him?

Yes, Molly told herself. As long as she didn't see Worth, life would resume its normal course. Or would it? Almost five years had gone by and never a day passed she didn't think of him. Residing in his house made a bad thing worse.

Right now she didn't have a choice.

As if he realized he wasn't alone, Worth swung around. When he saw who it was, his eyes widened, then a door seemed to slide over those eyes, blanking out his expression.

"Didn't anyone ever tell you it was rude to sneak up on a person?"

Go to hell.

She didn't say that, but oh, how she wanted to. To speak her mind in that manner, however, would only incite a verbal riot, and she didn't want that. Too much was at stake. She merely wanted to talk to him in a civil manner.

"Sorry," Molly finally said in a moderate tone.

"No, you're not."

She hadn't meant to sneak up on him without warning. She just happened to walk by the door leading onto the porch and saw him there, a booted foot propped on one of the iron chairs. He seemed to have been staring into the waning sun, far in the distance, as though deep in thought.

Molly guessed she should have coughed, or done something to reveal her presence, only she hadn't thought about it. She had just walked onto the porch and waited, seeing this as an opportunity she couldn't pass up.

"Look, Worth, I don't want to fight with you," she said at last. She'd meant what she'd said, too, especially when she watched him set the empty beer bottle down on the table, making more noise than he should have, which spoke volumes about his mood.

She couldn't let Worth see the effect he had on her. Not now. Not ever. And entering into another verbal skirmish with him would put the power in his hands, power that could end up destroying her and what she held dear. At all costs, she had to maintain her cool.

"Is that what we're doing?"

"I don't want to play word games with you, either."

He jammed his hands into his pockets which pulled the fabric tighter across his privates. For a moment, her gaze lingered on the mound behind the zipper. Then realizing what she was doing, she jerked her head back up to his face, praying that he hadn't noticed anything amiss.

If he had, he didn't acknowledge it. Instead, he continued to stare at her through those blank eyes.

"What do you want, then?"

"To take my mother's place."

His head bolted back at the same time he went slack-jawed. "As my housekeeper?"

"Yes," Molly said with punch in her tone.

He pitched back his head and laughed. "Get real."

"I'm serious, Worth," she countered with an edge in her tone.

"So am I, and that's not going to happen."

"Why not?"

He smirked. "Come on, Molly, you know why not. You're a nurse, and that's what you need to be doing."

"I can do both. I can take care of the house and my mother."

"What about Trent?"

"I'll put him in day care, and he'll be just fine."

"No."

She ignored that terse rejection and went on, "My mother's mind is her own worst enemy right now. She thinks you're going to replace her."

"That's hogwash. She has a job here as long as she wants one. And I'll tell her that."

"I appreciate that, but I still want to take her place. I can take care of Mom, encourage her and she will see that my job as housekeeper is temporary. This way she won't worry about someone permanently replacing her. She'll know I'm only filling in. Not only that, but I'm good. I grew up helping her clean houses."

Worth looked astounded. "Are you nuts? Besides, you don't have to do that anymore."

"I know I don't have to. I want to."

"Dammit, woman, you haven't changed a bit."

Molly raised her eyebrows. "Oh?"

"Yeah, you're still as stubborn as a mule."

She wanted to smile but didn't. Instead she held her ground. "So are you."

Worth cursed at the same time their eyes collided then held tighter than magnets.

Suddenly the oxygen in the air seemed to disappear, forcing Molly to struggle for her next breath. She could tell Worth was also affected as his face lost what little color it had left. And something else happened, too, though she couldn't identify it.

What it *hadn't* been was hostility. So had it been blatant desire? No. She'd been mistaken. He despised her and that wasn't about to change. She didn't want it to, either, she assured herself quickly, though the undertow of his sexy charisma was pulling on her.

Forcing her panic aside, Molly sucked in a deep breath and stared at him with an imploring expression.

"I'll think about it," Worth muttered on a sour note, cramming his hands further down in his pockets, which pulled his jeans even tighter across that area.

Molly averted her gaze and muttered, "Thank you."

He laughed, but again without humor.

Feeling heat rush into her face, Molly knew she should leave before insult was added to injury. She was about to do just that when his next words froze her in her tracks.

"Why did you run out on me?"

Five

She whipped back around and stared at him, feeling as though she were strangling. "What did you say?" she finally managed to asked.

"Don't play the deaf ear thing on me." Worth's tone was low and rough. "It won't work. You heard every word I said."

"I used to admire your badass attitude," Molly responded with fire. "In fact, I thought you were the stud of all studs because of it."

His eyebrows shot up as though that shocked him.

"But now I know better."

His features darkened. "Oh?"

"That attitude sucks big time."

The look that crossed Worth's face was chilling, and he took a step toward her, only to stop suddenly as though he were a puppet on a string and someone had jerked that string. She knew better. Worth was no one's puppet and never had been. Then she recanted that thought. His parents apparently knew how to pull his strings and get away with it.

"You know I really don't give a tinker's damn what you think about me or my attitude." Worth's voice had grown rougher.

"Then why ask me that question?"

"Curiosity is the only thing I can figure," he said in an acid tone, fingering an unruly strand of light hair that grazed his forehead.

Molly was suddenly tempted to reach out and push it back in place, something she had done on many occasions that long-ago summer. That sensual memory was so vivid she felt like a piece of broken glass was slicing through her heart.

"Your curiosity can go to hell. I'm *not* answering you."

He smirked. "That's because you don't have a satisfactory explanation."

"I have no intention of swimming through the muddy waters of the past. With your cynical judgment of me, I'd just be wasting my time anyway."

No doubt she was on the defensive and probably sounded as cynical as he did, but she didn't care. If she were going to survive and keep her secret from him and his parents, she had to best him at his own game, or at least match him.

Or she'd die in that muddy water.

"What's wrong?" His eyes consumed her. "You look like something suddenly spooked you."

Was that genuine concern she heard in his voice? Of course not. As before, her mind was playing tricks on her. He didn't give a damn about her. He was too much into himself.

"I'm fine," she bit out.

"Liar."

Her head kicked back. "What do you want from me, Worth?"

"What if I said *you?*"

Molly shook her head, trying to recover from the effect those words spoken in that toe-curling, sexy drawl had on her.

"I wouldn't believe you," she finally whispered.

Those dark pools roamed over her while the blood pounded in her ears like a drum. Oh, God, this kind of craziness had to stop or she'd be like putty in his hands again and wouldn't be good for any thing or any one. That was why she hadn't wanted to see him again. She was too weak, too vulnerable where he was concerned. She only had to be in the same room with him and she almost went to pieces.

"You're right, you shouldn't believe me," he said harshly and coldly, "because it's not true."

Molly sucked in her breath and tried to pretend that piece of glass hadn't taken another chunk out of her heart.

"Maybe you'll answer me this."

Molly barely heard him as she was striving to hold onto her wits and dignity under his attack, knowing that she should turn around and walk away, that nothing good would ever evolve from this conversation.

Why bother? She no longer gave a damn, either.

She simply didn't want to reconnect with that part of her life. Not only was it over and done with, it was way too painful to rehash, especially with him. What she and Worth had between them that summer was obviously dead, and to pull the past out of the dark into the daylight was futility at its highest degree.

"I have to go," she said in a halting voice, refusing to look at him.

"Do you love him?"

Shock caused Molly to blink. "Who?"

"Your husband. That Bailey guy who fathered your child."

Oh, dear Lord, if only she'd kept on going, hadn't sought him out on the porch, then they wouldn't be having this insane dialogue, making a bad situation worse.

"Yes," she lied.

His gaze dropped to her left hand. "Are you still married? I don't see a wedding ring."

"We're divorced." She hated lying, but right now it seemed her only recourse. He was like the Energizer Bunny; he just kept on going, kept on asking questions that were, frankly, none of his business.

If she didn't take charge, there might not be an end to his questioning. The more he knew, the more dangerous her presence became. And she was trapped. She couldn't leave because of her mother.

So they had no alternative but to work through their animosity toward each other, so she could remain on the ranch, ideally as his housekeeper. Maybe getting it all out in the open now, once and for all, was best for both of them. Then they could move on with the day-to-day grind of their lives and be less apt to meddle in each other's.

"I could ask you why *you're* not married," Molly blurted out of the blue, then was appalled. All she was doing was adding fuel to an already out-of-control fire. Would she ever learn to keep her mouth shut?

"Yeah, you could."

Silence.

"So why aren't you?" She paused. "I understand you're still seeing Olivia. I thought she would've dragged you down the aisle by now."

"Well, you thought wrong," he declared flatly, glaring at her.

Good. She'd finally hit him where it hurt, as he'd done to her so many times. Then she felt badly. She was above playing these hurtful games. Exchanging barbs only made the situation worse.

"If I'm going to stay here and work—"

"I haven't said you could do that yet," Worth interrupted, narrowing his eyes on her.

"I'm not leaving, Worth. I can't. My mother needs me."

He shrugged. "When it comes down to it, I really don't give a damn what you do."

"As long as I...we stay out of your way," she added, positive she had verbally expressed what he hadn't.

"You got it."

Ignoring the suppressed anger in his voice, she asked, "How about we call a truce? Do you think that's possible?"

"Do you?" His eyes were brooding.

"I'm willing to try."

He shrugged again, his eyes roaming over her, seeming to linger on his favorite spot—her breasts, which upped her heartbeat significantly.

"Whatever," he said without enthusiasm.

Molly gritted her teeth, but swallowed her sharp comeback. "Good night, Worth."

He didn't respond.

"I hope you sleep well," she added.

"Yeah, right," he muttered tersely, then turned his back on her.

Feeling the cold night air close in on her, Molly went back into the warm house, only to reach her room and notice that she couldn't seem to stop shaking.

"Hey, boss, what's up?"

Instead of going back inside the house, Worth had made his way to the barn. He hadn't expected to run into his foreman Art Downing, but then he shouldn't have been surprised. Art never seemed to know when to go home. He loved his job, especially caring for and working with Worth's stable of prime horseflesh. In fact, Worth had determined long ago that Art was more comfortable at the ranch than he was at home with his wife and kids.

Like him, maybe Art just wasn't cut out for family life.

"I was about to ask the same thing," Worth said.

Art lifted his massive shoulders that matched the massive girth around his stomach, and grinned. "Just making sure these beauties are settled in for the night."

All the while he talked, Art was busy rubbing one of the horse's noses.

"They're fine. Go on and get out of here."

"I will as soon as I check one more thing."

"And just what would that be?" Worth asked, glad to have something on his mind besides Molly who spelled trouble with capital letters.

"Making sure everything's ready for tomorrow's delivery."

Worth had bought another stud horse last week and the targeted arrival was the following morning. "Who you kiddin', man? You've had things ready since we bought him."

"You're right there." Art grinned, then rubbed his belly. "I am gettin' kind of hungry."

"Then get your rear home. And don't come back until it's daylight, you hear?"

"Yes, sir." Art tipped his hat then was gone.

Worth knew he might as well be talking to the air. His foreman would be here long before daylight, which made him more valuable to Worth than money could ever buy.

If he did as his parents wished and ran for political office, his time at the ranch would be limited. Thanks to Art, the ranch would continue to run smoothly.

After taking his own tour of the stables and rubbing all the horses and calling them by name, Worth made his way back to the house. Once there, he grabbed another beer out of the fridge, then headed to his suite. Glancing at his watch, he noticed he only had thirty minutes before he was due at Olivia's. She didn't like anyone to be late.

Dammit, he didn't want to go, not to a dinner party. Hell,

he'd just taken her to dinner the night before. However, he had made a commitment he couldn't break, especially as the gathering was designed to introduce him as a possible candidate for the Texas Senate. Still, it was too formal an affair for him. He knew Olivia expected him to dress for the occasion, which meant a sports coat and slacks.

He hadn't told her that wasn't going to happen. He planned on showing up in jeans, a white shirt and a leather jacket. If she didn't like it, that was her problem.

Instead of showering and changing his clothes, however, Worth plopped down on the side of the bed and guzzled half his beer. God, he was mentally tired, and he didn't know why.

Yeah, you do.

Molly.

Sparring with her on the porch had depleted his energy. He didn't know if he could take having her around here indefinitely, especially if she was working as his housekeeper. How ludicrous was that, anyway? So why had he mealy-mouthed around? He should have told her in no uncertain terms that was impossible.

But seeing her again had reopened the wound he thought had scabbed over. He supposed that was what he found most crippling. And frightening. With her arrival, it was like the messy tracks she had left on his heart had suddenly been covered by a lovely snowfall.

Which made him more of a fool than he'd thought. When it came to her, he couldn't use good judgment, and that made him madder than hell. At this point, he didn't need the aggravation of her presence back in his life.

Maybe if she'd still been married and brought her husband with her that would have made things easier. Like hell, he told himself with a snort, bolting off the bed and finishing his beer.

For a second he was tempted to grab another one and

maybe another after that. By then he'd be on his way to getting smashed. The thought of Olivia's reaction to him showing up three sheets to the wind brought a smile to his face.

Then he sobered. Right now he had nothing to smile about. Okay, Molly had upset his apple cart, so to speak, and he wasn't happy about that. But he remained king of this empire. No one told him what to do or how to do it.

So why had he suddenly gone soft?

The first time he'd laid eyes on Molly, she had managed to wrap him around her little finger. But after she had run off, married someone else and had his kid, Worth was so sure he'd feel nothing but contempt for her, if and when he ever saw her again.

Well, the contempt was sure as hell there, but so was another ingredient—an ingredient he refused to name, though it burned like a raging fire in his gut.

"Give it a rest, Cavanaugh," he muttered in a fierce tone, hurrying into the bathroom like a stampede of bulls were after him.

Only problem was, his mind refused to cooperate. In the shower, he squinched his eyes closed under the water, but it didn't help. Instantly, the image of Molly jumped to the forefront of his mind. She was standing in front of him, her eyes gleaming with desire, while she caressed his face, then his body.

Worth groaned, then gave in to the pain that momentarily paralyzed him.

Six

"Mommy, when can I ride a horse?"

Molly pursed her lips. "Oh, honey, I don't think that's going to happen."

Trent scrunched his face. "You promised."

"I beg your pardon, my sweet, but I did no such thing."

"I bet that man will let me."

Molly almost smiled. "Are you talking about Worth?"

"No, that other man."

Molly thought for a moment, then realized Trent was talking about Art, Worth's foreman. She had always thought he was such a nice man and that Worth was lucky to have him, especially when Worth would get upset about something. Art never seemed to take it personally. Instead he would listen, then take care of the situation.

"I saw him on one of the horses from Granna's window." Trent's voice held excitement.

"That's great, but you don't know a thing about riding a horse."

"I could learn," Trent said with a protruding lower lip.

"We'll see, okay?"

"I—"

She gave him one of her looks. "I said we'll see."

Although he didn't respond, Molly knew he wanted to. His lower lip was now protruding and trembling. "I'll talk to Mr. Art tomorrow, but I'm still not making any promises, young man. Is that clear?"

Trent's face instantly changed, and he ran and gave her a hug.

"Come on, big boy, it's time for your bath, then bed."

Again, Trent looked as if he wanted to argue, only he didn't, as though he realized he'd pushed his mother far enough.

Long after Trent was in bed Molly stood at the window, staring at the cantaloupe-shaped moon and Venus close by. What a lovely clear night, she thought. And chilly, too. She turned and glanced thankfully at the gas logs with their bright, perky flames.

Considering the way Worth felt about her, he sure had given her nice quarters. But then the entire ranch house was nice, built for guests and entertaining, which, now that she was old enough to think about it, rather surprised her. Worth wasn't the entertaining type, didn't have that personality, or at least not the Worth she'd known and loved.

Apparently, that Worth was no longer in existence. If anything, he was more self-centered, more spoiled than ever, an entity unto himself, definitely someone she no longer recognized or wanted anything to do with.

On second thought perhaps now she was seeing the *real* Worth Cavanaugh. Maybe back then, she'd been so young, so impressionable, so inexperienced, she simply hadn't recognized those flaws.

Besides, she'd been madly, and obviously *blindly,* in love.

Since that was no longer the case, she had to do what was necessary for her mother, then leave ASAP.

Thinking about her mother suddenly made Molly long to see her. She checked on Trent one more time, then went to Maxine's room. Thankfully, her mother was still awake.

After she had made both of them a cup of flavored decaffeinated tea, Molly eased into the chair by the bed and said without preamble, "I plan to enroll Trent in a day care facility in town."

"What on earth for?" Maxine asked in an astonished voice.

Molly hesitated, which gave her mother time to voice her displeasure.

"Since you're not going to be here long, I want Trent to stay here." Maxine struggled to sit further up in bed, then winced from the exertion.

Molly hurried to her side only to have her mother hold out her hand. "I'm okay. The sooner I learn to move on my own the sooner I can get up and get back to work."

"That's not going to happen any time soon, Mother, and you know it."

"I know no such thing."

"Please, let's not argue about that again."

"Who's arguing?"

A short silence followed her mother's succinct words.

"So back to why you want to put Trent in day care," Maxine said.

"I'm staying."

When Molly's bluntly spoken words soaked in, Maxine gave a start. "What does that mean?"

"It means that I'm not leaving any time soon."

"But I don't understand. What about your job?"

"For now, I have a new one."

Maxine's eyes widened. "Pray tell, girl, you're not making a lick of sense. What are you talking about?"

"I'm going to take your place here as housekeeper."

Maxine gasped. "No, you're not."

"Mother."

"Don't you Mother me in that tone, young lady."

Molly almost swallowed her tongue to keep from making a sharp retort.

Not so with Maxine. She hammered on, "Why do you think I worked my fingers to the bone all these years?" When Molly would have spoken, Maxine held up her hand again. "No. You hear me out. I did that so you wouldn't have to do manual labor, though don't get me wrong, working for Worth is wonderful. The best job I've ever had, not to mention he's the best person I've ever worked for."

Boy, did that admission ever surprise Molly. She would have thought the opposite, but then maybe it was when he was around her that Worth took on a different personality. No doubt, he abhorred the ground she walked on. Well, the feeling was mutual.

Liar, her conscience whispered before she shoved that thought aside and concentrated on what her mother was saying.

"But that doesn't mean I want you doing that kind of work."

"I'm not above doing that kind of work, as you call it," Molly said flatly. "I'm quite good at it, actually, since I grew up helping, and learning, from you."

"That's beside the point." Maxine glared at her. "I'd rather Worth fire me and hire someone else than for you to give up your job in Houston."

"I never said I was giving up my job. I'm just taking my sick leave and vacation time. Once you get your brace and start physical therapy, you'll be good as new in no time. Then I'll be out of here."

Her mother grunted in disbelief, then said with despair in her tone, "I'm afraid I'll never be the same again. What if those twisted muscles don't straighten out and I have to have surgery? If that happens, then I won't be able to walk across the room without a cane or walker. Worth will surely replace me then."

"There you go borrowing trouble again."

"No, I'm just being realistic, something you young people are not."

Molly rolled her eyes in frustration. "Talk about me being hardheaded."

"If I can no longer cut it," Maxine argued, "then what's to keep him from making me second in command?"

"Mom, we've been over this issue several times already."

"I know, and I'm sorry for beating that dead horse," Maxine said in a petulant tone.

"If I take your place, your job won't be in jeopardy."

"No matter. I'm not about to let you do that."

"Too late," Molly said flatly. "It's a done deal."

"I can't believe Worth would approve that. I need to talk to him."

"I'll admit he wasn't overjoyed at the prospect, but I think he'll come around."

"After I get through with him, he won't," Maxine said.

"This is between Worth and me, Mother."

"Please, Molly, don't do this." Maxine's tone had a begging edge to it.

Molly sat on the bed beside Maxine, leaned over and kissed her on the cheek. "Please, *let* me do this. Don't fight me. You've always been there for me, never judged me for shaming you by getting pregnant before I married, then immediately divorcing. It's my turn now to pay you back."

Maxine placed her palms on either side of Molly's face, looked into her face with tear-filled eyes and said in a torn voice, "You're my child, my baby. That's what mothers do—love unconditionally."

Molly fought back the tears. "And that is what daughters do, too."

Maxine dropped her hands and fell back against the pillow. For a long moment both were silent, seemingly lost in their own thoughts.

Maxine was the first to speak. "I thought you were going to marry Worth, you know." Her mother's voice was weak and far off.

Molly almost choked on the pain that suddenly squeezed her heart. "I did, too, Mom, only it didn't work out."

"You never told me what happened." Her mother's eyes drilled her.

Molly licked her dry lips. "I know."

"It's okay." Maxine reached out and grabbed one of her daughter's hands. "If you ever want to tell me about it, I'm here. I've never been one to pry and I'm not about to start now. You've got a precious child and a wonderful career, so it's best to let sleeping dogs lie."

Molly tasted a tear. "You've been the best mother ever and still are." She sniffled, then smiled. "Perhaps one day I'll be able to confide in you."

"But it's okay between you and Worth now, right?" Maxine asked with concern. "I guess what I'm asking is do you still care about him in that way?"

"Absolutely not," Molly responded vehemently. "Granted, we'll never be friends, but we're okay around each other."

Here she was lying to her mother again. But she couldn't help it. Once she had almost blurted out the truth concerning her and Worth, but the words had stuck in her throat. After that, she had talked with a minister in Houston when she'd found out she was pregnant, then entered counseling.

While some people might judge her harshly for her silence concerning the baby's father and fact that she'd lied about marriage, she felt her mother never would, even if she were to learn the truth. Still, there was a part of Molly that just couldn't unburden her heart to her mother, or anyone else.

For now, no loved one or friend was privy to her heart's secrets.

"My, but you're quiet all of a sudden."

Molly shook her head and said, "Sorry." Then she leaned her head sideways and added, "Have you thought about going to a facility while you're recuperating?"

"Have you gone daft, child?"

Molly chuckled. "No, but I had to ask."

"If I have to leave this place, I would go to Houston with you."

"That's certainly an option."

"Only not now. I want to stay right here, get well, then go back to the job I love."

Molly stood and gave a thumbs up. "Together we'll make that happen."

"I knew you were stubborn—" Maxine's voice played out with a forlorn smile.

Molly chuckled again. "I'm going to bed. We both need our rest."

However, when she returned to her room the sound of a car door slamming pulled Molly up short. Without thinking, she dashed to the window, knowing it was Worth returning from another night out. Probably with Olivia again, though she didn't know that for sure. Still, she didn't move, continuing to track his movements, hoping he couldn't see her because the room was practically dark. Only a small lamp burned in one corner.

Molly glanced at the clock on the bookshelves and saw that it was past midnight. If he'd been with Olivia, had they made love? Suddenly her stomach clenched. The thought of his hands and mouth caressing another woman like they had hers didn't bear thinking about. In fact, it made her flat outright sick to her stomach, which was in itself *sick*.

Of course, he'd made love to Olivia, if not other women, as well. After all, it had been almost five years since she'd seen him. A man like Worth, with a heightened sexual appetite, or at least it had been that way with her, wouldn't have remained celibate all that time.

Dammit, it didn't matter, she told herself. But it did, though she was loathe to admit it because such an admission was dangerous to her peace of mind and threatened her sanity.

If she was going to go through with her plan to work for him—and she was—then she'd have to corral her mind and not let it wander down forbidden paths.

When Molly realized she had been indulging, she blinked just in time to see him saunter toward the house. He was halfway there when he looked up at her bedroom.

Feeling her heart leap into her throat, Molly jumped back, out of sight. Had she been in time? Had he seen her watching him? If so, what must he think?

When she mustered up the nerve to peek again, he was gone. Then disgusted with herself and her juvenile antics, she mentally kicked her backside all the way to bed.

She heard the grandfather clock in the hall chime three o'clock, realizing she had yet to close her eyes.

Damn him!

He had seen her all right. And for a second he was tempted to say to hell with everything, stride inside and bound down the hall to her room. Then what? he asked himself.

Make mad, passionate love to her?

Sure thing, as if she'd let him cross the threshold much less touch her. God, what was he thinking when he let his mind and emotions have free rein? Dwelling on the impossible was crazy. More to the point, it made *him* crazy.

Why he hadn't sent her packing was beyond him. It wasn't too late, he reminded himself as he grabbed a beer, then made his way to his room, making sure he didn't pause in front of hers.

But sleep was impossible. He'd already had too much to drink. He'd used the boring dinner party as an excuse to get partially plastered, much to Olivia's chagrin. Boring though it was, something good had come out of it. The man Olivia had invited as a potential backer for his campaign turned out to be someone he'd instantly liked and to whom he could relate.

Ben Gibbs seemed to have felt the same way about him. They had talked at length, and Worth had come away from the conversation positive Gibbs would back him if he chose to run against the incumbent. He had also spoken highly of Worth's parents, which was another good thing.

Other than Gibbs, the rest of the evening had been only tolerable. After everyone had left, Olivia had wanted him to stay. He made up some lame excuse, which didn't sit well with her, and left.

Now, alone in his bed with only his tormented thoughts, Worth almost wished he'd spent the night with Olivia, so he wouldn't think about *Molly* and that kid of hers. For some reason, he couldn't get the boy off his mind.

If only *he'd* gotten Molly pregnant that summer day in the barn when he hadn't used protection, how different his life would've been. He'd have a child—a son no less.

Now, he'd probably never have that opportunity even if he wanted it. According to the doctor, he'd be damn lucky if he could father a child. A horse had kicked him in the groin shortly after Molly had run out on him.

At the time, he'd been so busy nursing his anger and bitterness against Molly the diagnosis hadn't registered.

Having anything to do with a woman after that had been disgusting to him. The emotional wounds Molly had left had been open and oozing.

Now, after having seen her son, the enormity and repercussions of his accident rose up and hit him in the face like the chill from a bucket of ice water. To make matters worse, he hadn't even told his parents. To this day, they still didn't know that he might not ever give them the grandchildren they so coveted.

Dammit, by all rights Trent should have been his.

"You're full of it, too, Cavanaugh," he said out loud, followed by an ugly laugh.

He drained the remainder of his beer, then tossed the empty bottle on the floor at the same time the room swam. Good. Maybe he was drunk enough to fall asleep. Without removing his clothes, he fell across the bed, trying to forget he was nursing a hard on.

For Molly.

Seven

"Mommy, these pancakes are so good."

"I'm glad, honey, but don't you think you've had enough?" Molly smiled at her son. "Five is a lot, even for a growing boy. But you do need to finish your milk."

"Your cakes taste just like Granna's."

Noticing that Trent's mouth was smeared with syrup and butter, Molly grabbed a paper towel, moistened it, then wiped his entire face, while he squirmed. "Be still. You can't go to day care dirty."

"I'm not dirty."

"Yes, you are," she corrected him with a broader smile. "Go brush your teeth, then we'll go."

"Where's he going?"

Stunned that Worth had pulled her stunt and made an appearance without her knowledge sent her heart into a tailspin. Striving to cover that fact, Molly pulled in a deep breath, and looked at him, which only added to her trepidation. It looked as though he'd just gotten out of the shower as his thick hair was still damp and slightly unruly, which always made her want to run her hands through it.

But it was what he had on that had her heart in such a dither. His flannel shirt was tucked into worn jeans that fit his long, muscled legs like a second skin, especially over his crotch, leaving nothing to the imagination.

For a moment her eyes honed in on that private area and set up camp. Then realizing what she was doing, she jerked her head up at the same time she felt heat flood her face.

To make matters worse, she knew what he was thinking. The lines around his mouth deepened, his eyes turned into banked down coals of desire. Their gazes met and held for what seemed an eternity, but in reality was only seconds.

Bless Trent. He was the one who broke the tension that sizzled between them.

"Hey, Worth."

Her son's words brought Molly back to reality with a thud. "Mr. Cavanaugh to you, young man."

"It's okay. He can call me Worth. I want him to."

Trent turned his eyes tentatively to his mother, as if seeking her approval. "Whatever," she said without conviction.

"I love your cows and horses," Trent said to Worth. "I wish I could ride one of your horses," he added down in the mouth.

"Trent." Molly's tone was reprimanding.

Trent pawed the tile floor with a booted foot, his lower lip beginning to stick out. "I didn't do nothing, Mommy."

"He sure didn't." Worth squatted in front of him. "How 'bout I start teaching you to ride today?"

"No," Molly exclaimed in horror.

Both looked at her like she'd just sprouted two heads.

"I'm about to take Trent to day care."

"Why?" Worth asked, standing, his gaze pinning hers.

Though she wanted to squirm, she didn't. She met him eye for eye. "Because I can't see about him and the house, too. And Mother's not able."

"Kathy can watch him."

"I need her to help me."

A grim look crossed Worth's face, especially his lips. "I don't want you doing that."

Molly glanced over at Trent, then back to Worth, as if to say now's not the time to have this discussion."

"Mommy?"

Without taking her eyes off Worth, she said to her son, "Run brush your teeth."

After looking from one adult to the other, Trent trudged off, his little shoulders slumped.

"He's not a happy camper," Worth said into the tension-filled silence.

"He'll get over it."

"Let him stay here, Molly. I'll hire someone to watch him."

"I can't allow that."

"Why the hell not?"

"I'm responsible for running the house—your house—and I don't want to be worried about Trent and what he's into. Furthermore, it's not your place to hire someone to watch my son."

"For God's sake, Molly, that's all the more reason to put an end to this nonsense. I don't want you running my house."

"Are you backing out on your word, Worth?" She glared at him.

His eyes narrowed on her. "Unlike you, I don't do that."

She wasn't stupid; she knew where that remark originated. He had just taken another potshot at her for when she'd walked out on him. "Contrary to what you might think, I don't do that, either."

He sneered, then muttered something under his breath.

She didn't want to know what it was because it would add coals to an already smoldering fire that simmered between them. Until her mother was up and about, Molly reminded herself she must contain her tongue and hold her counsel, or else she wouldn't survive this jungle she'd reentered.

"I was serious when I offered to teach him to ride," Worth said in a more conciliatory tone than she'd heard in a while. "But I was more serious about him staying here."

Fear burgeoned inside her. "Why do you care?"

"He seems to be a good boy, and I know how much Maxine enjoys his company. She talks about him all the time, how much she misses seeing him."

"My mother told you that?"

"You act shocked," he remarked in a dry voice.

"I guess I am." Molly's tone was confused.

"Obviously you don't know it, but I have a great deal of respect for your mother. She's not just my housekeeper. She's a friend and part of my family."

"I appreciate that, Worth," Molly said in a halting voice as she shifted her gaze. "I really do. I know she feels the same about you."

"That she does."

"Again, I so appreciate your patience with her injury."

"When she hurt her back," Worth responded, "her mind must've conjured up the worst possible case scenario because I never had any intention of letting her go."

"She definitely went into the panic mode."

"Under those circumstances, my suggestion is that you spend time working with, and caring for, her, and let the house go."

"I can't do that, Worth. Even though I'm a nurse, and a good one I might add, I'm not a physical therapist. Too, it wouldn't be good for Mother and me to be together that much. Too much togetherness can be a bad thing."

"Don't I know that," he muttered again.

"Speaking of togetherness, how are Eva and Ted?" Not that she cared, she told herself, stunned that she'd even inquired.

Worth shrugged and gave her a strange look. "Same as always—great."

"I'm glad," Molly acknowledged in a stiff tone.

"You never did like them and still don't." A flat statement of fact.

Molly deliberately changed the subject. "When I get back from town, I need to talk to you about upcoming events. I know about the day-to-day run-of-the-mill things. Mom told me your schedule, more or less, that you—"

"Dammit, Molly, put a stopper in it, okay?"

Her mouth clamped shut at the same time her temper flared. "Don't you dare talk to me like that."

"Sorry," he muttered again, shoving a hand through his hair, clearly indicating his irritation.

"Look, Worth, we can't go on like this."

"And how is that?"

"You're being deliberately obtuse, but for the moment I'm going to let that pass."

Worth eyes darkened on her. "Okay, you win."

Molly's breathing slightly accelerated. "On both Mother and Trent?"

"On one."

"And that is?"

"The house."

Her anger rose. "You have nothing to say about Trent."

"Don't you want him here?"

"Of course," she admittedly tersely.

"Then let him stay. I know someone who's perfect to look after him."

"And I'll pay them," she said in an unbending tone.

After having said that, she experienced a hollow feeling in the pit of her stomach like she'd done something terribly wrong and didn't know how to fix it.

Worth and Trent should not be a pair, but if she continued to remain unmovable, then it might raise a red flag, giving Worth cause for thought. She couldn't allow that. Hence, she'd try Worth's plan. If it didn't work out, then she could always insist on reverting to *her* plan and to hell with what Worth said or thought.

"That's fine by me," he said on a sigh.

"So can we get down to other business now?" she asked.

He made a face, then peered at his watch. "Now's not a good time for me. I have to meet with a breeder. How 'bout later, maybe this evening?"

Before you go see your lover. I don't think so. Appalled at her catty thoughts, Molly felt the color drain from her face as she turned quickly around, praying that he hadn't read her thoughts through her eyes.

"Molly?"

The crusty edge in his voice brought her eyes back around. "What?"

For another long moment, their gazes held.

Worth cleared his throat, then said in an even crustier tone. "Will that be okay?"

"I guess so," she responded in brittle tone.

Worth gave her another long look out of suddenly vacant eyes, then left the room. Once alone, Molly sank against the kitchen cabinet for support, wondering how she was going to survive staying there even one more day.

He just couldn't keep a lid on it.

It was as though he'd suddenly developed diarrhea of the mouth. He shouldn't have interfered with her plan to put the kid in day care. The last thing he wanted was to be saddled with her brat.

Not true.

He liked the boy, and that was the problem. He should leave them both alone, have as little to do with them as possible. Only that wasn't *possible* since Molly insisted on working for him.

Damn her lovely hide.

Only she wasn't to blame. He could have put his foot down and said an emphatic *no* and meant it. She wouldn't have had a choice but to comply. After all, she was on his turf with no alternative but to do as he said.

But again, he'd wimped out, and let her have her way, at least on one account.

Worth let go of a string of expletives that did little to relieve that gnawing in his gut. If only she didn't look so good or smell so good, having her around would be easier.

This morning when he'd walked into the kitchen and saw her dressed in those low cut tight black jeans that hugged her butt and legs to perfection, and the white T-shirt that also hugged her breasts and stomach with the same perfection, he wanted to grab her and punish her with hard, angry kisses for the havoc she was wreaking in his life.

Of course, he hadn't made such an insane move, didn't plan to, either. He aimed to keep as wide a berth between them as possible. With that kind of rationale, he'd be fine, or so he hoped. To think she'd only been there four days. That already seemed an eternity.

Realizing he was almost at his parents' house, Worth gave his head a fierce shake to clear it. Molly was poison and he had to stop thinking about her, *stop wanting her.* Around his parents, he had to be constantly on guard; they were much too inquisitive and much too intuitive.

They had never liked her and had made that quite clear. But he hadn't given a damn. He'd liked her. Hell, he'd *loved her,* and would have married her if she hadn't left him.

Bitterness rose in the back of Worth's throat in the form of bile. Swallowing deliberately, he concentrated on maneuvering up the circular drive in front of his parent's antebellum home. About that time, his father walked onto the porch.

Olivia's father, Peyton Blackburn, stepped out, too, just as Worth braked his truck, killed the engine and got out.

He didn't have anything against Blackburn except that he thought he was better than most, but then that seemed a characteristic of many of the well-to-do families in this town. He was sure people said the same about him and his parents.

"Hey, son, your timing's perfect."

At sixty Ted Cavanaugh still posed a striking figure, Worth thought. Tall and slender with a thatch of silver hair and blue eyes, his good looks had turned many ladies' heads. But as far as Worth knew, he'd never looked at another woman besides his mother. From all appearances, they seemed to adore each other.

"What's up, Dad?" Worth asked, then let his gaze wander to Olivia's dad who posed an unstriking figure. Blackburn, in his middle sixties, looked his age, sporting a paunch around the middle and deep grooves in his face. But the main reason Worth thought him unattractive was the scowl that rarely left his face.

Even now, when he appeared to be smiling, he wasn't. Yet when he spoke, his voice was pleasant enough. "We're working a deal, young man," he said to Worth. "It concerns you."

Worth paused, shook Peyton's outstretched hand, then patted his dad on the shoulder. "How so?"

Ted smiled a huge smile and was about to speak when Peyton jumped in. "No, let me tell him."

"Suit yourself," Ted exclaimed in an amicable tone.

"Tell me what?" Worth was curious and it showed.

"I've decided to go ahead and deed Olivia that parcel of land that adjoins yours."

Good for Olivia, Worth wanted to say, but didn't. What he did say was, "That's great, but what does that have to do with me?"

Ted and Peyton both looked at each other, then back at him, stunned expressions on their faces.

"What?" Worth pressed, getting more agitated by the moment.

"It's got everything to do with you, son, since you're going to marry Olivia."

Worth felt his jaw go slack.

Eight

"Dad, we need to talk."

Worth knew his blunt words bordered on rudeness, especially since he'd totally ignored Ted Cavanaugh's comment about marriage. But he didn't give a damn. Who he married was none of his parents' business, and he wasn't about to let them think it was—rude or not.

Blackburn shifted as though uncomfortable, then said, "Ah, look, I'll leave you two alone. I know you've got lots to discuss, especially with all this political stuff brewing."

"Thanks for stopping by, buddy," Ted responded absently.

Blackburn tipped the brim of his hat to both men, then spoke to Worth, "You take care, you hear? We'll talk about the land and the race later."

"Thanks, Peyton," Worth said, "we'll keep in touch."

Once he'd driven off, Ted said, "Come on in. Your mother's waiting to see you. I think she's made breakfast."

"Mother cooking?" Worth asked in a light voice, purposely masking the fury that was churning inside him.

"Hannah's on vacation," Ted said by way of explanation. "Anyway, we figured you'd be by, so…"

Worth's father let the rest of the sentence trail off as they made their way inside, straight to the kitchen, where the smell of bacon and sausage put Worth's stomach on edge. His mother was in the process of setting the table. When they entered, Eva looked up and smiled, then walked over and gave Worth a cool peck on the cheek.

Like his father, she didn't look her age, continuing to hold her beauty. Although tall and rather strapping, she had beautiful skin and hair, hair that held its true color, a natural blond. But there was an air about Eva that was also off-putting.

"You're shocked, I know," she said, waving her hand across the bar where an array of food was set.

"You got that right. How long has it been since you've made a meal?"

"I'd rather not say," Eva replied in a coy tone. "If you don't mind, that is."

Although she smiled, Worth noticed it never quite reached her eyes. Suddenly Molly's face rose to the forefront of his mind. When she smiled, every feature lit.

Now where the hell had that come from? Dammit, Molly should be the furthest thing from his mind.

"Get a plate and chow down, son, then we'll talk."

The last thing Worth wanted to do was chow down. After the comment his father had made in front of Blackburn, his stomach remained in no mood to tolerate food, even if it smelled divine. In order not to hurt his mother's feelings, he filled a plate and forced himself to swallow as much as he dared.

A while later, after the plates had been cleared and the cups refilled with freshly brewed coffee, Ted asked, "Did I open my mouth and insert my foot in front of Blackburn?"

Worth didn't pull any punches. "You sure as hell did."

Eva's eyes sprang from one to the other. "What's going on?"

Ted told her what he'd said.

Her eyes drilled her son. "I don't see anything wrong with that. You do intend to marry Olivia, don't you?" She paused, then went on before Worth could answer. "Although I am surprised she doesn't have a ring and that a date hasn't been set."

Worth barely managed to keep a lid on his temper. "Marriage is not in the cards for me," he said, "at least not any time soon." Probably never, he wanted to add, but didn't. No use throwing gasoline on a burning fire.

"And just why not?" Eva pressed in an irritated tone. "To be a more viable candidate for office, you need a suitable wife. And Olivia is certainly that."

That lid was jarring loose. "Don't you think that's my call, Mother?"

"What about the land?" Ted chimed in. "I thought you wanted to increase the size of your herd of horses."

A vein in Worth's neck beat overtime. "I do, Dad."

Had his parents always been this steeped in his business and he just hadn't realized it? If so, perhaps that was because he was an only child, and they doted on him. No excuse. He refused to let them live their lives through him.

"Look, Art and I are trying to figure out a way to utilize the land I already have," Worth explained. "We're not there yet, but we're making headway."

"Why would you do that when more land is being offered on a silver platter?" Eva asked in that same irritated tone.

"Because I'm not ready to marry Olivia."

"If your tone of voice is anything to judge by, you won't ever be."

"That's entirely possible," Worth quipped.

His parents looked at each other, then back at him. But again, it was his mother who spoke. "Is it because *she's* back?"

Here we go again, Worth thought with disgust. Same song, second verse. "No, it's not because Molly's back."

"I just don't understand you, Worth." Eva's tone was as cold as the look she gave him.

He refused to take the bait, so he kept quiet.

Eva's generous lips thinned. "You know we're concerned. You should respect that."

"That's right, son, you're not being fair to us."

Worth stood abruptly. "The fact that Molly has come to see about her mother is none of your business."

Eva's gaze tracked him. "I still can't believe you'd let her back in your house after what she did to you."

This time Worth's lips thinned. "Don't press it, Mother. I told you Molly's off-limits."

He might as well have been talking to the wall for Eva steamrolled right on, "You never said how long she plans to stay."

"Mother!"

Eva's hand flew to her chest as though terribly offended. "That's a perfectly legitimate concern I would think."

"She's taking her mother's place as my housekeeper." Hell, he might as well drop the bomb now as later, and let the debris fall where it may.

Ted and Eva gasped simultaneously, then they both started talking at once, which turned into a bunch of gibberish.

Worth held up his hand. "Don't say another word, either of you. I've made my decision and it stands."

"As my son," Eva said with a quiver, "I gave you more credit than that."

"Sorry to disappoint."

"I understand she has a child."

Worth shrugged. "So she has a child."

"I can't imagine her with a brat."

That nixed it. Suddenly fury was an invisible malignancy that threatened to devour him. Yet somehow he managed not to throttle his own mother. "His name is Trent."

"Then he's with her." Eva pursed her lips.

"Yes," Worth said in a tired tone.

"You don't still care about her, do you?" Eva asked in a softer, gentler tone as though realizing she pushed as far as she could without completely alienating her son.

"No." Worth's voice was clipped. "If we don't change the subject, I'm out of here. Is that understood?"

Eva sighed as she cast another look at her husband who merely shrugged his shoulders as if to say, what choice do we have.

"So, Dad, do you really think I have a chance to win the Senate seat if I decide to toss my hat into the ring?"

Ted's heretofore glum features returned to life. "You betcha. Dan Elliot has lost his popularity with his constituents, which means you've got a clear shot at taking the nomination, if not the election."

Worth rubbed his chin in an idle fashion. "I guess the next step is to have a gathering of supporters and test the waters."

"Now you're talking, son," Eva put in. "Once you win that Senate seat, perhaps you'll become so addicted you'll keep right on climbing the political ladder."

"Hold on, Mom. I'm not even sure about this race, much less anything else."

"I think a barbecue would do for starters."

Worth thought a moment. "That sounds so trite and typical, but I guess that's still the best way to go."

"You need to get Maxine—" Eva paused midsentence,

then made a face. "Oh, dear, for a moment I forgot she's out of commission."

"Not a problem. I've got it covered."

Eva's mouth looked pinched. "Well, I doubt that Molly's capable—"

"Mother!"

"Sorry," she said, compressing her lips.

Worth knew she wasn't in the least sorry, but nonetheless she had the sense to let the subject drop. Suddenly he felt the urge to get out of his parents' house before he completely blew his temper and said things he'd regret, not that he had any intention of defending Molly because he didn't. Still, it bothered him that they looked on her as someone they had carte blanche to belittle and get by with it.

Since he had no intention of defending her, he had no alternative but to keep his mouth shut. He couldn't have it both ways.

Suddenly Worth felt like he'd stepped in a bed of quicksand and was being sucked under.

"Look, I gotta go," he said, lunging to his feet and heading for the door. Then he turned and said to his mother, "Thanks for breakfast. I'll be in touch."

By the time he reached his truck, he slammed his hand down on the top and cursed a blue streak.

Believe it or not she had been at the ranch a week. Since Maxine still needed her, she intended to stay on a while longer. To her relief, the last few days had passed uneventfully.

Molly had gone about her business of taking care of the household duties. With Trent content and happy, watched by a young lady named Tammy Evans, she was free to do what needed to be done. With Kathy's physical help and Maxine's verbal input, Molly was pleased.

The house was lovely and her mother had apparently taken

great pride in keeping it that way, which made things easy for Molly. In the beginning, she'd been leery of her temporary position. But after the first day, Molly realized she actually enjoyed doing something different.

Working with the public, especially the *ill* public, was a far cry from working with inanimate objects such as dishes and crystal. Cooking was the part she liked least, never having mastered that craft like her mother. But she guessed it didn't matter because Worth apparently hadn't wanted her to cook for him.

It seemed as if they had fallen into a pattern of avoiding each other, which was just fine with Molly. Oh, they passed in the hall and at those particular times, their gazes never failed to meet, then tangle. Most times she couldn't read his response unless his features were pinched in anger.

She knew he continued to resent her presence, but that couldn't be helped, she told herself as she went about slicing some fruit for lunch. But she knew sooner or later, they would have to talk, not only about the house, but about upcoming parties or events.

In fact, word had gotten around that a barbecue for potential political backers was on the horizon. In due time she supposed he would speak to her about that.

Meanwhile, she would continue to divide her time between her chores, her mother and her son, all of which were full-time jobs. However, she wasn't complaining; the setting was too perfect. Not only did she work inside, but she worked outside, as well. If she had a hobby, it was growing plants. And her green thumb was evident, especially at this time of year. The multileveled porch was ablaze with potted plants filled with vibrant fall colors.

Now, as she continued to slice the fruit, Molly gazed through the window into the bright sunlight, admiring her handiwork.

She wondered what Worth thought, or even if he'd noticed the added pots of plants.

"You've done a great job with the porch."

Molly's heart went wild. Was that mental telepathy or what? She swung around and faced Worth who looked like he'd been ridden hard and put up wet. The lines on his face seemed deeper; his hair was disheveled; his jeans, shirt and boots were covered in dust.

"What happened to you?" she blurted out.

"Art and I have been clearing land."

"Must have been some task."

"It was that and more."

"You look exhausted."

"I am. But it's nothing a shower and a glass of tea won't cure."

She immediately crossed to the fridge and opened it.

"You don't have to wait on me, you know?" His voice was low with a moody edge to it.

She looked back at him, then swallowed. "I know, but I don't mind." Before he could say anything else, she latched on to the pitcher of tea, poured him a glass, then held it out to him.

As though careful not to touch her, he took the glass, then without taking his gaze off hers, put it to his lips and took a big gulp. His stare was all consuming.

Molly wanted to look away, but couldn't. She was mesmerized by the unexpected heat in his eyes and the way he smelled—manly—like clean sweat. Suddenly her palms went clammy and her mouth went dry.

Before he realized the impact he had on her, she whirled around, went back to the cabinet, picked up the knife and began cutting more fruit. It was in a split second that it happened.

The knife slipped and instead of slicing the apple, it sliced her. "Oh!" she cried, just as Worth reached her side, grabbed her finger, and squeezed it until the blood stopped.

"Dammit, Molly," he said in ragged voice.

"Why are you yelling at me?" she cried, looking at him only to realize his lips were merely a heartbeat away from hers, his eyes seemingly dark with need.

She knew in that second he intended to kiss her.

Nine

Only he didn't.

Worth swore, then focused his attention back to her finger that he now held under the faucet, rinsing off the blood. Molly looked on in shocked silence—not because she'd injured herself, but because she had wanted him to kiss her. Disappointment washed through her in waves.

No! her conscience cried. That was insane. She never wanted him to touch her. Physical contact of that nature was forbidden and out of the question. Again, keeping her distance was her only method of survival.

And her hand in his was *not* keeping her distance.

"It's okay," she murmured, tugging at her hand, only he wouldn't let go.

He grabbed a paper towel and gently touched the wound.

"Ouch," Molly exclaimed before she thought.

"Sorry." Though Worth's tone was gruff, his touch was

gentle, which made her quiver all over, especially since he continued to examine the wound at close quarters. Much too close.

When he finally raised his head and looked at her, Molly was hit with a sizzle of electricity. For a second the world seemed to tip on its axis. Clearing his throat, Worth moved his head back.

"I think you're going to live," he said in a husky tone.

Molly managed a shaky smile. "You think so?"

A semblance of a smile reached his lips, which warmed her insides even more. God, she couldn't let herself fall under this man's spell again. She couldn't. It was just too painful. He ripped her soul out once already and stomped on it. She couldn't allow him to do it again. If it were just her—maybe she'd go for it. But it wasn't just about her.

Trent.

He was the one she had to think about. With that sobering thought, Molly jerked her hand out of his, which in turn dislodged the tissue, causing the cut to start bleeding again. Without thinking, she stuck that finger in her mouth.

"Don't do that," Worth all but snapped.

She removed her finger and stared at him. "A little blood never hurt anyone."

"I'll get some ointment and a Band-Aid."

"That's okay. It'll eventually stop bleeding."

"Until it does, what are you going to do?"

She couldn't believe they were having this rather inane conversation about a cut that was certainly not serious. A big to-do about nothing, actually. "Ah, good question," she said at last.

"I'll be right back."

After he had gone, Molly wrapped another paper towel around the wound and leaned against the cabinet, realizing her legs suddenly had the consistency of Jell-O.

As promised, Worth returned in record time and without asking, reached for her hand. If he held her hand a bit longer than necessary to administer first aid, they both chose to ignore it.

Maybe that was because Trent came dashing through the door about that time, only to pull up short, his eyes widening on the scene before him. Instantly, Molly reclaimed her hand and stepped a safe distance from Worth.

Trent's eyes went straight to the bandage. "Mommy, did you hurt your hand?"

"Yes, honey, I did, but it's okay."

"Did Worth fix it?"

Molly forced a smile. "He surely did."

"But you're a nurse."

Worth chuckled, which instantly drew her gaze and made her catch her breath. It had been so long since she'd heard him laugh, her body went into meltdown. He was sex personified, and she couldn't stop herself from reacting no matter how hard she tried. If she weren't careful, she'd be drooling, for heaven's sake.

"You'll learn one day," Worth said to Trent, "that nurses and doctors are the worst patients ever."

Trent's eyes got big again. "Really?"

Worth winked at him. "Really."

"Okay, you two, enough," Molly put in, then focused on Trent. "Go wash your hands. Lunch is almost ready."

Trent hesitated, cutting his gaze to Worth. "Will you eat with us?" he asked.

Stunned at her son's bluntness, Molly immediately said, "I'm sure Worth has other plans. I'll—"

"No, I don't, except to wash up a bit."

Silence fell over the room at the same time Molly darted her eyes back to Worth. He returned her gaze with one as innocent as a new born babe's. Damn, she thought, now what?

She had planned to take her mother lunch, and she and Trent would join her while she ate. Worth had certainly usurped those plans. Not necessarily, she told herself. She could say no to Worth, tell him what she'd had in mind. If the truth be known, he was probably wishing he'd kept his mouth shut. Wonder why he hadn't?

"Oh, boy," Trent said, racing for a chair.

"Hey, slow down," Molly reprimanded. "You know not to run in the house. Any house."

"Sorry," he muttered, his eyes on Worth, who once again had something akin to a smile on his face.

Trent smiled back and Molly's stomach did a somersault. For a brief moment the resemblance between father and son was so obvious she could scarcely breathe, anxiety having another field day with her stomach.

"Molly?"

Worth's voice brought her out of her trance. "What?" Even though she answered, she knew she didn't sound like herself.

"Are you all right?"

"I'm fine," she said stiffly, groping to cover her tracks. "Why do you ask?"

Worth's dark eyes narrowed, but then he shrugged, glancing quickly at Trent whose eyes were ping-ponging between them, as if sensing something was going on.

"No reason," Worth finally said, then changing the subject asked, "What's for lunch?"

"Roast sandwiches, chips and fruit."

Worth winked at Trent. "Sounds like a winner to me. How 'bout you, son?"

Son.

Don't call him that, Molly wanted to scream. He's not your son—he's *mine*. All mine, she told herself savagely and desperately, as she looked out the kitchen window into the meadow, the sun creating a beauty that miraculously calmed her fractured nerves.

"Mommy, I'm hungry."

"Ah, sorry, honey. I'm coming."

Worth shoved back his chair and walked toward her. "Tell me what I can do."

"Nothing," she said in an obviously cold tone.

He paused midstride, his eyebrows kicking up and a scowl darkening his features. "Excuse me," he muttered, then pivoted on one foot and made his way back to the table.

Molly released a pent-up breath, knowing that Worth was not used to having someone give him orders. That was his job, and he expected everyone, especially hired help, to hop to it. The long hot days of their summer together taught her that.

However, for some unknown reason, he didn't make an issue out of her bossiness, most likely because Trent was there, which was a good thing. She wasn't in the mood to take any of his high-handedness.

"What do you guys want to drink?" Molly asked, making her tone as pleasant as possible, mostly for her own sake. She had to prove to herself that she could be with Worth and behave like a rational, in-control woman. No matter what, he must not rattle her.

Several minutes later, the goodies were on plates, on the table and the tea glasses filled. Though they ate in silence, Molly was aware of Worth, how much he turned her on and how much he provoked her. A double-edged sword, on which she hopefully wouldn't fall.

She sensed he was aware of her, as well. When she accidentally looked at him, he was watching her with a mixture of desire and anger.

"Mommy, I'm finished."

Thank God for her son's perfect timing. "I made cookies

for dessert," she said in a higher than normal voice. "You want one?"

"Can I have two?"

Molly cocked her head, then smiled. "I guess so, since you were such a good boy and ate all your sandwich."

"Mr. Worth, you want some, too?" Trent asked.

Molly couldn't help but notice that her son looked at Worth like he was a hero. She could understand that. As always, Worth looked the consummate cowboy, dressed in jeans, white shirt, and boots, and hat.

It was at that moment that she regretted letting Trent remain at the ranch. She should have insisted he go to day care, eliminating the chance of Worth and Trent becoming too chummy.

But it was too late to renege and too late for regrets. She'd just have to be sure to keep them apart as much as possible.

"You bet, I do," Worth said. "Who in their right mind would pass up homemade cookies?"

"Especially the ones my mommy makes." Trent grinned. "They're yummy."

"Thanks, sweetie," Molly said. "Before you dig in, why don't you and I take Granna's meal to her?"

"I want to stay here with Mr. Worth."

Worth raised his eyebrows. "Unless you need the help, we'll stay and eat our cookies."

Which was exactly what she didn't want. Since she'd seen the likeness in them, she couldn't bear the idea of leaving them alone together. Yet she couldn't make a scene about it, either. She might possibly raise a red flag, something she still did not want to do.

"That's fine," she muttered, grabbing her mother's tray and making her way out of the room.

Five minutes later she walked back in the kitchen to find

Worth seemingly hanging on every word Trent was saying. Panic almost paralyzed her, but she rebounded, saying to her son, "Hey you, it's your nap time with Granna."

"Aw, Mommy, I don't want to take a nap. I'm too big. Tammy doesn't make me."

"Since Tammy's off today, you're out of luck." Molly gave Trent a pointed look. "So don't start whining."

He made a face, which she ignored. "I'll join you and Granna in a minute, after I clean up the kitchen." Molly paused and ruffled his hair. "First, though, tell Worth bye."

Reluctantly, he did as he was told.

"See ya, fellow," Worth said. "Hey, how would you like to look at some of my horses, say maybe tomorrow?"

"Oh, boy," Trent shouted, his gaze landing on Molly. "Could I, Mommy? Could I?"

It was on the tip of her tongue to say not only no, but hell no. She didn't say either. "We'll see. Okay?"

Trent knew not to argue, but his reply was glum. "Okay."

Once he left, a silence fell over the room. At last, Worth broke it. "Come on, let's get this mess cleaned up."

"I don't need your help," Molly said in a stilted tone, then realizing how she must have sounded, she softened her next words. "But thanks, anyway."

"Suit yourself," Worth almost barked.

She turned her back and went to the sink, thinking he would leave, only to have him say, "When you finish, I'd like to talk to you."

Molly swung around, her breasts rising and falling rapidly.

For a millisecond, his gaze honed in on her chest, which created more chaos inside her. "Ah, can't you talk to me now?"

"No. I want your full attention." His tone was thick and low. "I'll be in the sunroom."

The entire time Molly cleaned up the kitchen, dread hung

over her. And panic. Had Trent said or done something that had made Worth suspicious? God, she hoped not. But Worth had sounded so serious she couldn't help but worry.

By the time she joined him, Molly was a bundle of nerves. "So what did you want?" she asked without preamble.

His eyes seemed like black holes as they pinned her, as though her directness pissed him off. "Sit down. Please."

"I'll stand, if you don't mind."

"If you're trying to test my patience, you're doing a damn good job of it."

"Sorry," she whispered, hoping for the best but preparing for the worst.

"I'm sure you've heard that I've been considering having a political rally here. Anyhow, I've decided to have it and I want to do a barbecue."

Feeling slightly shell-shocked, she peered into his face, knowing her eyes would rival the size of silver dollars. "Is that what you wanted to talk to me about?"

"Yes," he said in a clipped tone. "What else?"

"Ah, nothing. I'll take care of it."

"No, you won't."

"Excuse me?"

"I don't want you messing with all that. Hire someone to cater it."

"Why?"

"Because I said to."

They glared at each other.

"That's what I was hired to do."

He laughed without humor, which raised her ire to the next level. "If my mother were still in charge, would you hire an outsider?"

Worth didn't hesitate. "No."

"Point taken, I hope."

Faster than a streak of lightning on a stormy night, Worth crossed the room and grabbed her arm.

The very air around them seemed to have dried up, making speech impossible.

"Did anyone ever tell you you've got a smart mouth?" he asked.

"Let me go," she demanded.

"When I'm ready," he shot back.

Molly parted her lips just in time to collide with his mouth in a raw, wet, hungry kiss that sent her senses reeling. She clung to him for dear life.

Ten

From some foreign place in her mind, Molly heard Worth groan, then the next thing she knew he had shoved her at arm's length. With his breaths coming in shuddering gulps, he stared down at her, a dark, tortured expression on his face.

Molly couldn't move. She couldn't even breathe. Like him, she was too stunned at what had just taken place. Thank goodness, he hadn't abruptly released her, or she would have fallen to her knees. They were weak and trembling just like the rest of her body that still felt the imprint of his lips adhered to hers. To make matters worse, she continued to feel the way he'd pushed into her, making her aware of his hard and urgent mound. To her horror, it had felt so good, she had pressed back.

What on earth had she done? *The unpardonable.*

As though he read her mind, Worth muttered in a low, agonized tone, "I must have lost my mind."

Those cold, harsh words were the catalyst Molly needed

to strengthen her body and her resolve. She jerked herself free and gave him a bitter look. "How do you think I feel?" she flung back in much the same tone.

"Okay, so it was a mistake," Worth responded, his tone bordering on the brutal. "Still, I'm not going to apologize."

Molly laughed, but it, too, was crammed with bitterness. "You apologize? The great Worth Cavanaugh." She laid the sarcasm on so thick a sharp knife wouldn't have cut it. "Why, that thought never crossed my mind, not for one second."

"Dammit, Molly."

"Don't you dare damn me. You're the one who—" She stopped suddenly, hearing her voice—along with her control—crack. She could easily go to pieces right in front of his eyes. As it was, she was barely keeping body and soul together. But she couldn't let him know that. She feared he would use that weakness to his advantage.

After all, he was fighting on his home turf, which definitely gave him the upper hand.

"Kissed me," Worth finally said, finishing the sentence she'd started earlier.

"That's right," she countered with spunk.

"And I don't know why the hell, either."

"I hope you're not asking me."

"Maybe I am."

"You're wasting your time."

"I'm not so sure about that." He paused and their hostile gazes collided. "You damn sure kissed me back."

"That I did," she admitted, then felt heat seep into her face and scorch it. He was right. She had kissed him back. Had she ever, and even though it had been so long, Molly felt like she had just reentered the gates of heaven. But again, she didn't intend to share feelings so personal even she was having trouble digesting them.

She had tried so hard to keep from stepping into this hornets' nest and getting stung, but she had failed miserably. The truth was, she hadn't stepped in; she'd jumped in.

Jamming a hand through his already mussed up hair, Worth stepped further back, though he continued to stare at her under hooded eyes. "Maybe you shouldn't stay here."

Molly panicked, widening her eyes. "Are you kicking me out?"

"I didn't say that," he said tersely.

"Then exactly what did you say?"

"Dammit, Molly."

"That's the second time you've damned me."

He blinked.

"That's right, and I don't like it. It takes two to tango, Worth. So maybe you should stop damning me and take a look in the mirror."

She watched the color drain from his face as he took a step toward her, only to pull up short when Trent came bounding in.

"Mommy."

Her son certainly had a knack for timing, for which she was grateful. Reclaiming her composure was difficult, but she managed to do it. "What, honey?"

"Granna she needs you."

"I'll be right there."

"I'll go back and tell her."

Molly forced her gaze off Worth and onto her son. "No, that's not necessary. I'm on my way."

"Can I stay with Worth?" Trent asked out of the blue.

Worth's eyes darted to hers, a question in them.

"No, Trent," she said in a scolding tone. "You know better than to ask."

She felt Worth's gaze purposely pull at her. "It's okay. I don't mind if he comes with me."

"Well, I do."

"Mommy, please," Trent begged, pulling on her hand.

"I said no, Trent."

His chin began to wobble, but he didn't say anything. Instead, he turned and ran back down the hall.

No doubt about Worth's reaction to the rejection, either. His features were taut as their eyes sparred. "In that case, I'm outta here."

"No, please, wait."

He pulled up and whipped around, his jaw clenched, indicating he was pissed. Well, so was she, but they both had to get over this incident and move on, or else she *would* have to go.

"I'm waiting," he said in a ragged voice.

"We need to talk specifics about the barbecue."

He gave her an incredulous look. "You've got to be kidding me."

She ignored that, and enunciated her words very carefully. "No, I'm not kidding you."

"Look, I really don't give a damn about the particulars." His gaze held her captive. "Especially right now."

"You know," she spat, "you really can be a bastard."

"So I'm told."

"I'm not going to disappear."

He looked taken aback, then recovered. "What does that mean?"

"It means I'm not leaving." Her tone was soft yet her eyes drilled him. "Short of you kicking Trent and me out, that is."

A scowl twisted his features. "You make me sound like some kind of monster."

"No, I believe I said bastard."

He looked like he wanted to strangle her, probably thinking she'd crossed way over the line. Frankly, she didn't care what he thought. Even for Worth, his obnoxious behavior was a bit over the line.

She was about to make another suitable retort when she was interrupted by Trent.

"Mommy! Granna wants you. She says she's all hot."

"Go see about your mother," Worth said brusquely. "Let me know what's going on, and if she needs anything."

"Now, Mommy."

"I'm coming, son."

At the door, Worth turned. "Call if you need me."

Molly's eyebrows rose at the concern she heard in his voice, but didn't say anything.

"Later," he muttered and walked out.

Molly turned and practically ran to her mother's suite, certain something was wrong, making her feel badly about dallying with Worth. Suddenly, she wanted to yell at someone; she didn't care who. She'd known coming back here would be difficult. She just hadn't known how difficult until now, still feeling the brutal, yet hungry imprint of Worth's lips on hers.

What had she done?

"Mom, are you okay?" The instant Molly asked that question upon entering Maxine's room, she knew the answer. Her mother's face was extremely red, like she'd been stung by fire ants.

Without saying anything further, Molly raced into the bathroom, grabbed a rag and wet it with cold water. Then racing back into the room, she bathed her mother's face. Then she folded the cloth and laid it across Maxine's forehead.

On the beside table was a bottle of Tylenol. She grabbed two tablets, then proceeded to give them to her mother.

"Mom, do you hurt anywhere, like your stomach, for instance?"

"No," Maxine responded weakly. "Just tired."

"I'm calling the doctor. He may have to make a house call."

Five minutes later she was off the phone, assured that if Dr. Coleman was needed, he'd be here, but that he thought Maxine had probably just picked up a bug and would be okay in twenty-four hours or so.

Molly's thoughts ran along the same line, but she'd still wanted the doctor's opinion. By the time their conversation ended, Maxine felt less feverish, and she'd fallen asleep. However, Molly did not leave, choosing to remain in the sitting room with Trent in her lap, reading to him.

It was only after her mother's fever broke entirely and she was feeling much better that Molly left with Trent in tow to find Worth. Whether he liked it or not, she was determined to get his input concerning the upcoming barbecue, as well as her mother's. A week was not long to make plans, and her personality didn't lend itself to waiting until the last minute.

Besides, she wanted to make a good impression. Worth was convinced she couldn't do it. She was convinced she could. Another battle of wills. Besides, proving him wrong would certainly buoy her battered spirits.

"Mommy," Trent whispered, "I like Mr. Worth."

"I'm glad."

A moment of silence followed. "Why don't you like him?"

Molly's chest constricted, and she had no comeback.

She was the stubbornest, most hardheaded female he'd ever known. He'd thought Olivia had that top honor, but she couldn't hold a candle to Molly. After all these years, he had never quite figured her out. Maybe that was one of the reasons she still interested him.

"Get a life, Cavanaugh," he muttered savagely, kicking at a clod of dirt with the toe of his boot. He'd made the rounds of the stables, met with Art and was now heading to the new barn. He hated that his other one had burned down, but since it had, he'd built a state-of-the-art one this time.

It was his pride and joy, too. He loved to spend time there, and he loved to show it off. In fact, he would like to live in it. If he were truly a free spirit, he could move in and be perfectly content.

He liked his home, too. After all, he'd designed and built the sprawling ranch house with the help of Art and several subcontractors. But again, there was something unique about the barn. Perhaps that was because it was spacious and smelled of hay and horseflesh.

Whatever the reason, the massive structure—painted red, of course—had become a sanctuary when he needed it. Like now.

It would be a perfect place to have his barbecue. Thinking about that stopped him in his tracks, and he muttered a curse. He'd been excited about entertaining until Molly took over the housekeeping duties.

The thought of her working as a maid still soured his stomach.

She should have been his wife, not his housekeeper. Suddenly, he upped his pace, like the seat of his pants was on fire.

By the time he made it to the barn, his heart was pounding unusually hard, though he prided himself on being in great physical shape. Emotionally, though, he was a cripple—thanks to Molly. She apparently still had the power to turn him like a combination lock, thus exposing his emotions so easily.

He gritted his teeth, picked up the nearby pitchfork, and began spreading hay that didn't need spreading. But he needed something to do with the overabundance of energy raging inside him.

He'd lost his mind.

That was the problem. He'd kissed her. Hell, he hadn't just kissed her; his mouth had practically raped hers, especially when he'd felt the lush roundness of her breasts poking his chest. To make matters worse, his hands had dropped to her hips so that she'd feel his arousal, which made it even harder to let her go.

She'd tasted so incredibly good, smelled so incredibly good, felt so incredibly good that he'd lost all perspective, his body wanting a satisfaction it wasn't getting.

Just when he'd realized what he was doing and was about to thrust her away, she had gone limp in his arms, and had begun returning his wet, savage kisses. She'd even gone so far as to entwine her tongue with his.

Yet he'd eventually done what he'd had to do and that was to put her at arm's length. But that small endeavor took every ounce of fortitude he had in him.

Looking back on it now, he didn't know how he'd done it. Without thinking, his eyes dipped south and he let an oath rip. Whenever he thought about her, or she was around, he went hard. Somehow he had to figure out a way to stop this crazy rush of blood to his groin.

Maybe what he needed was Olivia. She could give him what he wanted in the way of sex. But the thought of touching her after Molly was repulsive and not going to happen.

That added to his fury and frustration. How dare she come back into his life, wagging some other man's kid, and tormenting him this way?

How dare *he* let her?

Eleven

"Mom, how are you feeling?"

Her mother tried to sit up. Molly placed a hand on her shoulder and stopped her. "Don't. I'll do the sitting."

"I'm fine."

Molly rolled her eyes. "Yeah, right."

"Don't use that high-handed tone with me, young lady." Maxine's smile took the sting out of her words.

"Yes, ma'am," Molly countered with mock severity at the same time she felt her mother's forehead and it was indeed cool to the touch.

"See, I told you I was fine. My fever's gone."

Molly smiled her relief. "Guess it was just a twenty-four hour bug, after all."

"Where's Trent?" Maxine asked, looking around.

"He's with Tammy, running around outside."

"My, but that boy seems to have taken to this place like ducks to water."

Molly gave Maxine a suspicious look. "Don't let those wheels of your mind turn in that direction."

Maxine huffed, as though insulted. "I don't know what you're talking about."

"Damn straight you do."

"Why, Molly Bailey, I don't recall ever hearing you say that word."

"I don't often." Molly paused for emphasis. "Unless it's called for, or I need to make a point."

Maxine picked at the blanket on the bed. "So what's wrong with me wanting you and Trent closer?"

Feeling like a terrible daughter, Molly clasped Maxine's hand. "Nothing, Mom, nothing at all."

"Then why won't you consider it?"

"Why don't you consider moving to Houston?"

Maxine went stark-eyed. "And leave Worth?"

"Yes, and leave Worth," Molly replied in a pointed tone.

"Why, he…he wouldn't know what to do without me," Maxine stammered, seemingly appalled that Molly would even think such a thing.

"I'm sure Eva and Ted would help him out."

Maxine narrowed her eyes. "My, but you sound bitter. What have they ever done to you?"

"Mom, look, I don't know how this discussion got started, but let's can it, shall we?"

Maxine looked taken aback and Molly sensed she'd probably hurt her mother's feelings, but she couldn't help it. At this point, she was doing well just to survive remaining on the ranch, especially after what had happened yesterday between her and Worth.

Because of that kiss, her heart remained sore to the touch. And to think she'd convinced herself that Worth couldn't cause her any more pain.

Apparently, she still had a lot to learn about herself.

"I didn't mean anything by that, Molly. Since you've been here, you've seemed different. Uptight might be the word I'm searching for."

"Mother—"

Maxine went on as if Molly hadn't spoken. "I know things didn't work out between you and Worth, and I hate that because I thought you two were crazy about each other."

She paused and took a breath. "And maybe things didn't turn out the way you wanted, getting married, then divorced, but that shouldn't have a bearing on your attitude toward Worth and his family. Frankly that puzzles me, because you don't have a mean-spirited bone in your body."

Before she found herself getting further tangled in that bed of thorns, Molly forced a laugh. "My, but you must be feeling better, Mother dear. I've never heard you deliver such a long speech."

"If you weren't grown, girl, I'd turn you over my lap and give you a good spanking."

Molly laughed for real this time and gave her mother a big kiss on the cheek. "I love you, even though you nose around where you don't belong."

"Huh! There you go, insulting me again."

"Oh, Mom, I'm okay. But you and this place have been a bit of a strain on me, I'll admit."

Maxine's features became whimsical for a moment. "I just wish I knew more about what makes you tick. You're my only child, but sometimes I feel like I don't know you at all."

"Mother, enough."

"Please, just let me get this off my chest, okay?"

Molly held her council.

"You were married and divorced, and I never even met the man."

"That's all water under the bridge."

"To you, maybe, but not to me. He was Trent's father, for Pete's sake. And I don't even know him." Maxine's words ended on a wail.

Oh, but you do, Molly wanted to shout.

Instead, she grabbed her mother's hands, squeezed them, then peered closely in her eyes. "You and Trent mean more to me than anything or anyone else. I know I've brought you pain by not explaining everything to you. But one day, I promise I will. I just can't say when."

Maxine's eyes filled with tears as she squeezed Molly's hands even harder. "Until that day, I promise I'll try to keep my mouth shut and not bug you."

Molly grinned. "Bug me. Mmm, that sounds like you've been around your grandson."

"Speaking of my grandson," Maxine injected on a lighter note, "you've done a splendid job raising him."

"The raising's just getting started, actually."

"Well, so far, so good, my child."

"Thanks, Mom," Molly said in a slightly choked voice. "Now that you've mentioned that boy, I'd best go see about him. First though, there's a matter I need to discuss with you."

"Okay."

"Tell me how I go about planning a barbecue without any help from the host."

Maxine threw her head back and laughed. "First off, you don't ask him. He doesn't have a clue."

"I suspected that."

"Nor does he want one."

"I suspected that, too."

Maxine chuckled again, then sobered. "If only this old back would straighten up, I could have everything done in no time at all."

"Sorry, you're stuck working through me."

"Not to worry. We'll make a great team. It'll be a rally people will talk about for a long time."

"The gossip flavor of the month, huh?" Molly said with a twinge of bitter humor.

"That's right, honey."

Molly got off the bed, leaned over and kissed her mother's still cool forehead. I'll check on you later."

"Send Trent to see me."

"Will do."

Trent and Tammy were walking toward the house when Molly walked out the door. Trent ran to her. "Mommy, can we go to the barn?"

"Oh, Trent," she said with exasperation.

"You promised."

"I did no such thing."

"I saw Worth go in there, but Tammy wouldn't let me go."

"Tammy did the right thing."

The young girl smiled her sweet smile, showing off dimples that made a plain face almost pretty.

"Thank you for today, Tammy," Molly said. "We'll see you tomorrow."

"Yes, ma'am." She turned to Trent who was pouting. "See you, buddy."

"I'm not your buddy."

"Trent! Your manners."

"Sorry," he muttered.

Tammy merely smiled again, then strode off.

When Molly turned toward Trent again, he was making a beeline for the barn. Her anger flared. Since coming here, he'd turned into a wild child.

"Trent!" she called. "Stop right where you are."

He did, but ever so reluctantly. When he stared up at her, he had a belligerent look on his face. They were really going to have to sit down and have a talk. She couldn't allow his insubordination to continue unchallenged.

"Mommy, are you mad at me?"

"Yes, I am."

"I'm sorry.

"You should be," she said, catching up with him.

That was when she realized the barn was in sight. She pulled up short. Would Worth still be there?

"I don't wanna go back inside," Trent muttered, sounding down in the mouth.

Molly thought for a long minute instead of just blurting out, *too bad*, which turned out to be her downfall.

Trent grabbed her by the hand, "Please, don't make me."

"All right, you little scoundrel, you win. We'll go see what Worth's up to. Maybe he'll let you rub an animal."

"Oh, boy!" Trent jumped up and down. "Come on, let's hurry."

"Hold on. There's no need for that."

Still, it was an effort to keep up with her son. By the time they covered the remaining distance to the barn, Molly was out of breath. She grasped Trent's hand tighter in hers, stopping him.

He gazed up at her with a question in his eyes. "What?"

"We can't just go barreling in there like we've been invited because we haven't. That's not nice."

"I got invited yesterday," Trent said in his big-boy voice. "'Member, Mommy?"

"Ah, right." Molly paused, then digging for courage, she called out, "Worth, are you in there?"

"Yeah. Come on in."

The second she saw him, Molly stopped in her tracks, thinking how sexy he looked leaning on the pitchfork with several twigs of hay stuck in his hair. Sheer willpower kept her from walking over to him and pulling them out.

Totally unnerved, her body broke out in a cold sweat. She shouldn't have come here, especially not with him watching her with eyes that seemed to seduce her on the spot.

"Wow!" Trent said in awe, looking around.

Molly dragged her gaze off Worth and stared at the premises herself. "I second that wow."

"You like, huh?" Worth asked, clearing his husky voice.

"It's great." She took a chance and looked at him again. The desire had been tempered. Actually, his features were blank. "But what about the old one?"

"It burned."

Her voice transmitted her shock. "Burned?"

"To the ground."

"Aw, man," Trent said.

Her son's comment was lost as her mind slid back to that summer, to the old barn where they made love for the last time. She could tell from the change in Worth's features that he, too, was thinking about that day.

The day she'd gotten pregnant.

Feeling dizzy, she closed her eyes. When she opened them again, Trent and Worth had gone ahead.

After a few moments, Worth paused and turned. "You coming?"

"Where are we going?" she asked in a slightly quivering voice.

He stared at her for a long moment. "To show Trent some of my prize horseflesh."

"Okay."

She followed, but didn't really get into the scene like the two of them. After she'd seen several horses, they all started to look alike, with the exception of their color.

"I'm sorry if we're boring you."

Molly almost visibly jumped at Worth's rather harsh and unexpected voice, definitely taking umbrage to what he said. "I'm not bored."

His eyebrows shot up. "Couldn't have proved it by me."

"Mommy, aren't you having a good time?" Trent chimed in as they made their way back to the main section of the barn, as if sensing the sudden undercurrent that ran between the two adults.

"I'm having a great time, honey. Only it's time we head back to the house. I have to make dinner and you have to get a bath."

"Is your mother all right?" Worth asked, changing the subject.

"She's fine. I guess it was just a twenty-four hour virus."

"Again, anything she needs, you just let me know," Worth said almost fiercely. "Anything."

"Thanks," Molly said, thinking at least he thought a lot of her mother. Too bad… She slam-dunked that thought before it could take a life of its own.

Worth had rejected her, not the other way around. She had to keep that in mind.

"Hey, buddy, that's off-limits."

Worth's louder-than-usual voice jerked Molly back to the moment at hand to find Trent on the first rung of the ladder leading up to the hayloft.

"Trent!"

He froze.

"Don't you dare go a step further," Molly said. "You have no business up there."

Hanging his head, Trent turned around.

Molly grabbed his hand. "Come on, let's go."

When they made it to the door, she forced herself to look back at Worth who was once again leaning on the pitchfork, staring at her with that smirk of his. Ignoring him, she said, "I'm about to make supper. Will you be joining us?"

"Nope."

His gaze looked her up and down, which made her body grow hot. "I suppose you're going out again." God, what made her say that? Even to herself, her tone sounded waspish. And jealous. Dear Lord, what must he be thinking? Probably that she cared about what he did, which couldn't be further from the truth.

His eyes burned into hers. "As a matter of fact, I am."

"Fine," she said in a prim tone, then walked out, silently cursing herself all the way back to the house.

"Ouch, Mommy!" Trent cried. "You're pulling my arm off."

"Be quiet, and keep up," she demanded, her breath coming in spurts.

Twelve

Molly almost wept with relief.

The shindig was in full swing without any glitches. *So far,* she reminded herself, tamping her excitement because things could change in the blink of an eye. The day after the debacle in the barn, Molly had finally pinned down Worth as to a date, time and guest list for the barbecue.

She couldn't have put the trimmings in place, of course, without her mother's help, especially since they'd had only a week to get ready. But that had been enough time since Maxine was a pro at planning last-minute parties.

As promised, she had directed traffic, so to speak, from her domain, as Molly fondly called her mother's suite.

Surprisingly, Maxine's back had improved much quicker than first expected. The brace and physical therapy combined seemed to be doing the trick. Molly was a bit disappointed, however, that Maxine couldn't join the festivities even for a little while. But the doctor had been afraid it might be too exerting, and Molly had agreed.

Now, as she looked around the premises, Molly was astounded at the number of people who had attended, just about everyone who had been invited. Yet Molly had been prepared. Her mother had warned her and she'd listened.

Most of the guests were now gathered on the multilevel porch, laughing and talking. At various points, tables were set up and decorated, awaiting the arrival of plates filled with all kinds of barbecued meat.

A band set up by the pool was doing its thing. The singer, belting out a country western song, had drawn a crowd. Other attendees were eating, drinking and being merry, which was exactly what the Cavanaughs wanted.

The hired help aimed to please.

Then kicking herself for that sarcastic thought, Molly forced her mind onto more pleasant things, such as the beauty that surrounded her. Yes, God had definitely smiled on the day. She looked up and didn't see one cloud in the sky.

Talk about great temperature. One couldn't have asked for better. Cool, but not cold—light jacket weather—perfect for an outside event.

Tammy was watching Trent, freeing Molly to take care of anything that might arise and might keep things from running smoothly. But she didn't mind the hard work. It kept her from thinking about Worth, looking at Worth and wondering about Worth.

Forbidden.

All the above fit into that category for her. Suddenly Molly felt a pang near her heart that she couldn't ignore. Stopping and closing her eyes, she took a deep, shuddering breath. When she opened them Worth was looking straight at her.

For an instant, she stood transfixed. He was leaning against a tree, seemingly totally relaxed, surrounded by several men who were talking non-stop—probably trying to convince him what a great politician he'd make.

She agreed.

As usual, he had on a starched white shirt, black jeans, dress boots and a George Strait Resistol. He was total eye candy, of which she couldn't seem to get enough.

Although she was sure he'd shaved that morning, his chiseled features no longer bore that out. He had the beginnings of a five o'clock shadow, which merely enhanced his sexy good looks.

Her heart began pounding like she'd been hiking a mile straight uphill. He broke loose from the posse and strode toward her, his gaze never wavering.

She wished she had the nerve, no, the willpower, to turn her back and pretend she hadn't seen him. Even though that wasn't going to happen, she nevertheless stiffened her spine, preparing herself for the worst.

The last few times their paths had crossed the exchanges between them hadn't been pleasant—anything but, actually.

It seemed as though every time he saw her, he was in an angry mood. Yet he looked at her with anything but anger. Desire and fire often lit his eyes, which kept her on edge. Despite the fact that he despised her, he wanted her. He didn't try to hide that. She suspected that was what kept his anger boiling.

She was sure today was no exception. By the time Worth reached her, his features looked like they were carved out of stone, though his tone was surprisingly soft. "Have you sat down at all?"

"No, but then, I'm not supposed to."

"Hogwash."

Her eyes widened.

He leaned in closer, which called attention to his cologne.

God, he smelled so good. For a moment, Molly's head spun, and she wanted to rest her head against his chest and say to hell with everything and everybody. Then reality hit her in the face, and she literally jumped back.

A dark frown covered Worth's features. "For heaven's sake, I'm not going to touch you."

"I know that," she snapped, crossing her hands over her short pink jacket that barely topped the waist of her low cut jeweled jeans. In doing that, she knew she'd slightly bared her waist as her white camisole underneath was also short. Even when Worth's eyes dropped there, and she saw desire heat his dark eyes, she made no effort to lower her arms.

"Then why did you jump?" His muttered question was spoken in a guttural tone.

"Does it matter?" she asked, thinking she should be ashamed of herself for purposely allowing him to see her naked flesh, knowing what it would do to him. What was happening to her? Once aroused, Worth was like a lighted stick of dynamite; he could go off at any moment.

Instead of that frightening her, it excited her.

As if he could read her thoughts, he stepped closer and whispered, "You'd best be careful how you look at me."

Color flooded Molly's face and she turned away, but not before saying, "Ah, I'd best get back to work."

"I want to talk to you."

She whipped back around, careful her facade was back in place and asked, "What about?"

"To tell you what a great job you've done on such short notice."

"Is that a thank-you?"

"You betcha."

His praise took her so by surprise that her mouth flew open. Her reaction brought an unexpected smile to his lips, which made her heart beat that much harder. It had been a long time since he'd smiled—or at least at her. It seemed as if the sun had broken through a dark cloud.

She smiled back.

He rolled his eyes, though his smile widened. "You're a piece of work, Molly Whoever."

She almost giggled at his unwillingness to say her last name, then caught herself, especially when their gazes tangled and held, while sexual tension danced all around them. For a breathless moment, he looked as if he might actually grab her and kiss her again.

She'd like nothing better.

Appalled anew at her thoughts, Molly shook her head at the same time he shook his, putting everything back on an even keel. "I'm glad everything's going well."

"That's because of you."

"And Mother."

"Of course."

For another moment silence surrounded them.

"I want you to sit down, even have a beer."

"Why, Worth Cavanaugh," she said in her most southern drawl, "you know that wouldn't be good 'cause I can't handle spirits all that well."

He threw back his head and laughed. "Don't I know that. The drunkest I've ever seen you was that night—"

As though he realized what he'd said and where this conversation was headed he broke off abruptly, a scowl replacing the laughter. "Dammit, Molly," he said in a savage tone, "you almost ruined my life."

She gave back as good as she got. "And you almost ruined mine."

Another silence.

"Hey, Cavanaugh, get over here. Rip wants to talk to you."

The moment was severed, never to be repaired. Without looking at her again, Worth turned and walked away. Thank God, a table was near by so she could sink onto the bench, or she might have sunk to her knees. Every bone in her body was quivering.

Every nerve.

Molly couldn't let him paralyze her. Wouldn't let him do that to her. The best antidote for her heavy heart was a dose of her child. Trent had a way of putting things back in perspective. Molly was well on her way to finding her son when she almost ran head-on into Eva and Ted Cavanaugh.

"Oh," she said in a faltering tone, quickly moving back. "Sorry."

Though Molly hadn't seen them since her return to the ranch—she'd purposely kept her distance at the barbecue, too—she knew sooner or later her luck would run out. The inevitable had happened. After her encounter with Worth, meeting them face-to-face couldn't have come at a worse possible time.

With them, there was no good time, she thought, feeling a pinch.

The intervening years had been kind to Eva. Oh, she was maybe a bit heavier and had a few gray hairs now mixed in with the blond, but amazingly her face remained virtually unlined. She still carried her large frame with the same confidence as always.

Aging had also been kind to Ted. He was still tall and good-looking, especially dressed in jeans and boots. She couldn't tell if he was losing his hair since he had on a Stetson.

"Hello, Molly," Eva said in her usual haughty tone, which had always irked Molly and still did.

Ted chimed in, "Yeah, Molly, it's good to see you."

Maybe he had a little too much enthusiasm in his voice to

suit Eva because she shot him one of *those* famous Eva looks, indicating he had done something to displease her. Molly knew that when it came to her just being on planet Earth was displeasing to Eva.

Once she had cared. Now she didn't. And the *didn't* felt damn good.

"I hope you two are well," Molly said out of politeness more than anything else.

Eva inclined her head and ran the tip of her tongue across her lower lip. "Do you really care how we are?"

No. As far as I'm concerned, you can butt a stump and die. Molly smiled her sweetest smile. "Of course."

"How much longer do you intend to stay here?"

"As long as it takes."

"For what?"

Eva knew, so Molly wasn't about to indulge her. Now that she was older and wiser and knew the vicious games these two played, she was not about to take a ticket. When the situation called for it, Molly could be a bitch, as well.

"Her mother, Eva," Ted put in, apparently embarrassed by his wife's open hostility.

"By the way, how is Maxine?" Eva asked, though her tone was devoid of empathy.

"You know very well how she is," Molly said without mincing words. "I'm sure Worth keeps you informed."

"Actually," Ted said, "we don't see that much of our son."

Although Molly was shocked at that disclosure, she didn't let it show. Besides, she felt a tad sorry for the elder Cavanaugh. When he was not with his wife, he was a nice man. That summer he'd treated her with dignity and respect until—

"I'm talking to you, Molly."

Molly clenched her hands to her side to keep from slapping both of Eva's cheeks. She was the rudest person she'd ever known and Molly would be damned if she apologized for woolgathering. "What did you say, Eva?"

"I said you're not wanted here."

"Eva!" Ted exclaimed, giving her a hard look. "Now's not the time for this kind of conversation."

"That's all right, Ted, I don't mind." Molly forced a smile. "Eva should feel free to say what she wants."

Eva laughed though it fell far short of humor. "Mmm, not the same cowed young girl you used to be, huh?"

"That's right."

Eva leaned in closer, her features hard. "Make no mistake, honey. You're no match for me and never will be."

"That thought never crossed my mind," Molly drawled in her sweetest tone yet.

Ted pulled on Eva's arm and said between his teeth, "Let it go, dammit."

Whipping her face around to her husband, Eva said, "If you don't like what I'm saying, you can leave." Her glare harshened. "But you ought to be right in here with me. For our son's sake, if nothing else."

"Eva," he said again with considerably less confidence, as though he knew he was fighting a bear using only a switch.

"It's all right, Ted." Molly gave him a real but halfhearted smile. "I'm no longer that young, stupid girl I once was. I can take care of myself."

"Molly, I'm sorry."

"Don't you dare apologize to her," Eva flung at him viciously.

Ted merely held up his hands, then stepped aside.

She'd had enough of Eva Cavanaugh, too, and was close to telling her so. Only her mother and her condition kept her quiet. She didn't think Worth would take any rash action like asking her, Molly, to leave, but when it came to his parents, she wasn't sure. That summer had taught her how much he depended on his parents and how much influence they had on him.

"Molly, one more thing."

"I'm listening, Eva," she said calmly, knowing that would get Eva more than anything else.

"I'm sure you know that Olivia and Worth are soon to be married."

"Not to worry, Eva." Molly smiled. "She's welcome to him. They'll make a perfect couple."

With that she walked off.

Thirteen

The party was winding down and for that Molly was grateful. She knew it had been a smashing success, if the mood of the guests was anything to judge by. Everyone seemed to have had their fill of the best barbecue in east Texas and all the booze they could want.

And the hottest band in the county was still playing.

The guests who remained behind were the really happy campers; her instincts told her they had talked Worth into finally throwing his hat into the political ring. Of course, she didn't know that for sure, not being privy to that information.

The way John Lipscomb, Worth's wannabe campaign manager, was slapping Worth on the back was the best indication that changes were in the works.

Molly still felt like Worth would make a good politician, not that her opinion mattered; it didn't. Still, after musing about it, she sensed he'd make a good one. He was such a take-charge person, one who made decisions and stuck to them. Honesty was another *must* quality. Despite his having been less than honest with her, she felt that didn't apply to his day-to-day dealings. In her book, a politician should have those assets and more.

A sigh split Molly's lips as she looked over the grounds and spotted a table with leftover debris scattered over it. She had just taken steps in that direction when a hand caught her arm.

Knowing that touch above all else, her heart lurched and she swung around to face Worth.

"How 'bout a dance?"

For a split second, shock rendered her speechless, then she stammered, "I…I don't think so."

"Why not?" Worth held on tightly, staring at her out of naked eyes.

"It wouldn't be appropriate," she whispered, feeling her insides go loose.

"Baloney."

"Worth."

"If you don't dance with me, it's because you don't want to."

"I—"

He didn't bother to let her finish the sentence. He grabbed her, pulled her close and they began to do the Texas two-step in perfect unison, which wasn't surprising. That summer they had danced many a time together, and Molly had reveled in each step. Perhaps that was because she was in his arms where she had longed to be.

Now, she'd just gotten into the beat of the music when the song abruptly ended.

"Damn," Worth muttered.

She wanted to mutter hallelujah, knowing they were being watched by the remaining guests, his parents and his lover. Not a good thing.

"Look, I need to get back to work."

"You know how that pisses me off."

"What?" she asked innocently.

"Telling me you have to work when you don't."

"Go ask Olivia to dance," Molly said in a weary tone, gently moving out of his arms, then she hurried to the table where the centerpiece was just short of becoming airborne. She had the object in hand when she felt the hairs on the back of her neck stand on end. Someone was behind her.

She whirled around and stared into the lovely face of a strange woman.

"I'm Olivia Blackburn," she said bluntly.

Molly schooled herself to show none of the myriad of emotions that charged through her. God, what had she done to deserve attention from both Worth's parents and his girl in one afternoon?

"Hello, Olivia," she said with forced politeness, having to admit that the woman was lovely in the truest sense of the word. Her hair was red with blond highlights, and her eyes were blue—a rare combination—but a stunning one, nonetheless. And she had a figure to die for. Though short and trim, she had oversized breasts that emphasized her tiny waist.

She would be just the right person on Worth's arm when he did his political thing.

"If you don't mind, we'll dispense with the pleasantries," Olivia said into the heavy silence, her tone nasty.

Molly took offense, but she kept her mouth shut. If Olivia had something else to say, then so be it. She couldn't care less, one way or the other.

"I know why you've come back."

Molly shrugged. "Good for you."

"You're fooling no one. It's for Worth."

"Oh, please," Molly exclaimed in disgust.

"When you two were dancing, I saw how you looked at him."

"Then you saw wrong."

"No way." Olivia's tone now reeked of sarcasm.

Molly sugar-coated her smile, then said, "Surely you noticed, he's the one who pulled me onto the dance floor."

That blunt statement seemed to rob Olivia of words, but only for a second. She rebounded with the force of an alley cat fighting for survival. "You're not wanted here."

"Trust me, I wouldn't be here, if I had a choice."

"Oh, I know you're saying you came back because of your mother, but I know better."

"Really, now." Molly made her tone as insulting as possible, plus she plastered on a fake smile, both of which seemed to spark Olivia's eyes.

"You're nothing but a slut, Molly Stewart, or whatever the hell your name is, and you'll never be otherwise."

"Now that you've gotten that off your chest, is there anything else?" Molly was determined to keep her voice stone-cold even. She wasn't about to let this vindictive witch rattle her cage.

Only she had, Molly admitted silently, feeling perilously close to tears and hating herself for it.

"As a matter of fact there is. Worth is mine, and I intend to marry him."

"Good for you."

Olivia smiled an evil smile. "You're not fooling me. You'll never get Worth back, so you might as well pack your bags, get your brat and leave town."

"Stop it!"

Olivia blinked, clearly taken aback by Molly's sharp tone and words. "Despite what you think, you're no better than me. As for my son, you leave him out of this." Molly took a heaving breath, then hammered on, "As for Worth, you're welcome to him." She paused again. "To my spoils, that is."

Olivia gasped while her hand flew to her chest as though she might be having a heart attack. While Molly didn't wish that, she was glad she'd pierced Olivia's hard heart with an arrow much the same as Olivia had pierced hers.

Olivia's recovery was quick. Stepping closer to Molly, she hissed, "No one talks to me like that and gets away with it. Trust me, you'll pay."

Molly didn't bother to respond. Instead, she whipped around and walked off, not even aware of where she was going until she reached the cool, shadowed barn. For a second, she was tempted to crawl into the loft and sob until she couldn't sob any more. But giving in to her heartache would only make her feel worse.

Suddenly she felt trapped, wanting to flee Sky, Texas so badly her stomach roiled. Leaning against a post, she surrendered to her pain, letting the tears flow.

"Are you okay?"

Fear froze her insides, especially when she realized her intruder was none other than Worth himself. After those rounds with his parents and his woman, *he* was the last person she wanted to see, especially since her face was saturated with tears.

Would this nightmare ever end?

Before she faced him, she dabbed with a tissue she fished out of her pocket. Maybe in the shadows, he wouldn't be able to tell she'd been crying.

Wrong.

"You're not okay," he said more to himself than to her, as he made his way further into the barn.

Panicked that he wouldn't stop until he was within touching distance of her, which she couldn't handle, Molly turned with her arms outstretched. "Don't."

Worth stopped instantly, though she knew taking orders from her, or anyone, went against his grain. Too bad. She'd had it with the entire Cavanaugh clan.

"Leave me alone, Worth," she said in a low voice, feeling drained to the core.

"No."

"No?"

"You heard me."

"I can't take any more," she said, hearing the crack in her voice and knowing he did, too.

He took two long steps, which put him within a hairs-breadth of her. However, he refrained from touching her.

"I know what's going down."

"I don't think you do."

"I'm not blind, Molly."

"It doesn't matter," she countered in a resigned tone.

"Mother and Dad cornered you." A flat statement of fact.

"I don't want to talk about it."

"Well, I do," he said flatly.

Silence.

"What did they say, dammit?"

Anger suddenly flared inside her. "In a nutshell, I should get lost."

He muttered some of the foulest words Molly had heard in a long time. "They don't speak for me."

"Couldn't prove that by me."

Ignoring that shot, he went on, "I also saw Olivia talking to you."

"She also told me to get lost, that you belonged to her."

Another string of curses flew out of his mouth, then he said, "Contrary to what she said, there's no wedding in the offing."

"Maybe there should be. She'll make the perfect politi-cian's wife—all show and no do."

That muscle in his jaw jerked, indicating that he hadn't liked her remark, but he didn't respond.

"I need to go," she whispered, feeling more drained by the moment.

"Despite what you think, they—Mother, Daddy, Olivia—don't speak for me."

"Like hell they don't," she said, whipping her head back and glowering at him. "From the outside looking in, it appears the monkeys run the zoo, not the zookeeper."

"Damn you, Molly." His nostrils flaring, he grasped her by the arms, hauled her against his chest and peered into her eyes.

"I told you not to touch me." Her teeth were clenched so tightly her jaw throbbed.

"Not in those words, you didn't."

"Then I'm telling you now."

"What if I like touching you?"

She struggled. "Let me go."

"No."

"Worth." Her voice broke.

"Worth what?" His also broke.

"This is crazy."

She swore she could see the blood heat up in his eyes as they held hers captive. "God, Molly, I can't think of anything but you."

"Stop it, please," she pleaded, fearing not so much what he would do but what she would do. Right now, she needed to be held and loved, having been battered and beat up since the moment she'd arrived.

Kindness towards her now would surely be her undoing. It would lead to the one thing she could only dream of, but never have.

Him.

"I can't," he whispered, his agony evident.

Then he did what Molly most feared. He sank his lips onto hers in what was a hot, savage kiss that seemed to rip her soul out of its socket. At first, she fought him, then when his tongue warred with hers, she lost all will and gave in.

As the kiss deepened, their bodies went slack until their knees met the floor of the barn. That was when she felt him reach under her camisole and cover a breast. She moaned and without thinking, dropped her hand to his zipper, feeling him enlarge under her hand.

"I want you," he muttered. "I have to have you. Now." It was when he began to unbutton her jeans that she came to her senses, crying out. "No. I can't do this."

One hard push was all it took for him to lose his balance and fall backward. That was all she needed to scramble to her feet and flee from the barn, his string of curse words following her.

She placed her hands over her ears and ran for dear life.

Fourteen

"Well, son, are you, or aren't you?"

Worth rubbed his stubbled chin. He had gotten up and come to his parents' place before he'd showered and shaved. He'd at least taken time to brush his teeth.

"How 'bout a cup of coffee first?" Worth asked, continuing to massage his prickly chin.

"Eva is the coffee brewed?" Ted called out from his place at the breakfast room table.

"Coming."

Worth still didn't know what the rush had been about to get over to his parents' ranch. His mother had called earlier and said they wanted to talk to him over coffee ASAP. He'd just rolled out of bed, bleary-eyed from having drunk too much the night before, trying to forget Molly was down the hall and that he wanted her more than he'd ever wanted anything in his life.

Yet, she was off limits to him.

Someone who gave her word then went back on it was something he couldn't get past or tolerate. Besides, he believed in the old adage that you can never go back and pick up where you left off. It almost never worked.

However, that didn't stop him from craving the pleasure of Molly's company in his bed. He nursed one particular whisker on his chin, letting his imagination run wild. If she were willing to have sex with him, what would it hurt? A good lay for old times' sake?

Wonder what Molly would think about that? He knew. She'd tell him to go straight to hell in a handbasket, and he wouldn't blame her. After all, he hadn't exactly made her stay at the ranch a bed of roses. In fact, he'd been a thorn in her side at almost every turn.

But dammit, she'd deserved it, he kept telling himself. Still, that didn't absolve his conscience, and he didn't like that. Guilt was not even a word in his vocabulary, and he wasn't about to add it now.

"Ah, thanks, Mom," he said, peering up when Eva set steaming mugs of coffee in front of him and his dad.

"Hannah made some scones and blueberry tarts, your favorites." Eva smiled as she leaned down and grazed her son's cheek. "I'm warming them even as I speak."

Worth shook his head with a frown. "Ah, Mom, thanks, but I'm not hungry."

"Sure you are," she said. "Or at least you will be when you smell them. I think they are Hannah's best efforts yet." She paused and smiled her confident smile. "And Lord knows she aims to please you. Above all."

If only his mother would stop her prattle. If not, Worth wasn't sure he could hang in for very much longer. His head was hurting like someone was beating on it with a jackhammer and his stomach was pitching. If he choked down even a morsel of food, and it stayed down, it'd be a bloody miracle.

But how could he tell his parents he'd gotten dog drunk because he wanted to sleep with a woman who had betrayed him, and whom they held in such contempt? He wouldn't, mainly because it was none of their damn business.

"So tell us what you're thinking."

"Yeah, right," Worth mumbled into his mug.

Eva's eagle eyes honed in on him, before saying bluntly, "You look dreadful."

He put his cup down and peered up at her. "Thanks."

"Well, you do."

"Thanks again." Sarcasm lowered Worth's voice.

"Don't play dumb, Worth," Eva said in a scolding tone.

He rolled his eyes. "Let it go, Mother. I'm not in the mood."

"When are you ever in the mood?"

"What the hell does that mean?"

Ted waved his hands. "Hey, you two, time-out. We're a family who's supposed to be civil, right?"

"I'm going after the goodies," Eva said, exasperation evident in her tone.

"Don't pay any attention to your mother," Ted said, his features scrunched in a frown. "She's obviously in one of her moods. It'll pass."

"It had better," Worth countered without mincing words. "I don't like her in my face, Dad."

Ted's lean face drained of color. "I know, son. Just bear with her. She only wants the best for you, and she thinks that's in politics."

"What if I don't agree?" Worth asked.

Eva walked back into the room and placed a plate of piping hot goodies in the middle of the table. Worth swallowed hard and tried not to look at them. Even the smell turned his stomach, but he decided to keep that to himself. Maybe later, he'd try a bite or two, to keep his mother off his back, if for no other reason.

"Want me to help your plate?" Eva asked with a smile, certain she'd won her son over.

"Not right now," Worth responded. "I'm still enjoying my coffee." Which was a lie. Right now, all he wanted was to go back to his ranch, shower and hit the sack.

"So back to what I asked earlier, son, have you made up your mind?"

Worth heard the anxious note in his father's voice and sighed. His mother, for the first time was quiet, as if holding her breath until he answered. "Nope."

Both gave him a stunned look.

"I can't believe you're still dallying," Eva said, anger deepening her voice. "Even though the rally was only yesterday, you still should make a decision."

"It's not that easy. For me it's a huge decision and a huge commitment."

"Why should that bother you now?" Ted asked, his brows drawn together in a frown. "You've never backed down from a challenge yet."

"You know my heart's really in expanding my horse business," Worth pointed out. "Both would be a bit much to tackle at the same time."

Eva flapped her hand. "The chance to breed horses will always be there. Your political chances won't."

"I'm well aware of that, Mother."

Eva's face took on a pinched look. "Are you also aware that if you don't hurry up and marry Olivia you might lose her?"

That was the straw that broke the camel's back. Worth lunged out of his chair, which caused his parents to jump. "I'm not marrying Olivia."

His mother's hand flew to her throat. "What?"

"You heard me."

"Not ever?" Eva asked, her voice coming out in a squeak.

"Not ever," Worth responded in a tired voice.

Silence filled the room for a moment while Eva and Ted stared at each other, their faces registering perplexity and dismay.

"It's her, isn't it?" Eva asked in an acid-filled tone.

Worth folded his arms across his chest. "I don't know what you're talking about."

"Like hell you don't."

"Eva," Ted said, glaring at his wife.

"Well, it's the truth. He hasn't been the same since Molly came back."

"Leave Molly out of this." Worth's tone brooked no argument. "And while we're on that subject, stay away from her. I know both you and Olivia took your shots at her at the barbecue." Worth transferred his gaze to his dad. "That goes for you, too."

Ted flushed while Eva ground her teeth together.

Finally Eva said, "We have every right—"

Worth cut her off. "You don't have any rights when it comes to speaking for me. Neither does Olivia."

"Worth, you're upsetting me," Eva said, "making me fear things that I shouldn't have to fear."

"If it has to do with Molly, you can stand down. Trust me, she hates me and can't wait to leave here."

Eva released a huge breath. "Thank God for small favors."

Worth drained his cup and put it down. "Thanks for the coffee."

"You mean you're leaving?" Eva demanded, wide-eyed.

"That's right. I'll talk to you later. Meanwhile, try to stay out of my life."

He didn't turn back around, but he knew both their mouths were gaped open.

* * *

Molly tiptoed into her mother's room that same afternoon and saw that Maxine was sleeping. She stood by the bed for a second and peered down at Maxine, feeling herself smile. Her mother was definitely on the mend.

The shots the doctor was injecting into her back had worked wonders. Of course, Maxine hadn't been released to do any housework yet. However, her mother was up and walking, alternating between a walker and a cane, which was a praise. It wouldn't be long now until Molly and Trent could leave.

Thinking of her son sent her to the window where she peered outside. She expected to see Tammy and Trent playing, and she did. What she didn't expect to see was Worth.

Only there he was. With them.

He was dressed in old jeans riding low on his hips, hugging his powerful legs and an old cutoff T-shirt that exposed his washboard belly and his navel. In truth, he was a gorgeous specimen.

And the effect on her was galvanizing as she watched the scene play out before her. Worth had brought a colt from the stable and was letting Trent rub on it. But it was Worth on whom she was concentrating.

As soon as possible, she had to get out of this house, out of *his* life for good, which meant she never intended to set foot on this ranch again. Her mother would just have to come and visit her.

Deciding the panacea to her tormented thoughts was work, she turned her back on the window. When called for, Molly could be a lean, mean, cleaning machine. Today was one of those days. Cleaning things, polishing things, making things sparkle not only occupied her mind, but her hands, as well.

Molly had just changed into some grungy jeans, and a T-shirt without benefit of a bra to encumber her efforts. She had pretty much cleaned the downstairs yesterday until it glowed. She felt the upstairs was entitled to the same treatment.

Suddenly, Molly paused in her thoughts, wondering if Worth had decided to run for office, or not. Of course, she would be the last to know unless he confided in her mother, which was possible.

She was delighted Worth and Maxine had such a good rapport. When the time came for her to leave, it would be with a clear conscience, knowing Worth would never let her mother want for anything.

Worth didn't like many people, but to the ones he did, he was loyal to a fault. She was grateful Maxine fit into the latter category.

She just wished she did.

"Can it," she spat out loud, then cut her gaze to the bed to see if her outburst had awakened Maxine. It hadn't. She turned then and went back to her room. The instant she walked in, her cell phone rang.

Surprised but glad at the caller, Molly said with enthusiasm, "Why, hello, Dr. Nutting."

"Hey, kiddo."

His familiarity was just the balm she needed for her battered senses. While he was the consummate elderly doctor in looks, with a thatch of white hair, delving blue eyes and an ever-ready smile, that wasn't his only claim to fame. He was one of the best and most renown doctors in the south, especially when it came to cardiology.

She'd been thrilled and honored when he'd chosen her as his head nurse. Now that he was willing to send her to school to become a physician's assistant, she was humbled and even more eager to please.

"I'm so glad to hear from you, Doctor."

"Same here, young lady." He paused. "So how are things?"

Molly gave him a quick rundown of her mother's condition.

"Ah, so you may be returning sooner rather than later."

"Sounds like you miss me," Molly said in a teasing tone.

"You have no idea. I've come to depend on you too much, I think."

Instantly Molly felt a bout of homesickness come over her. "Is everything going okay? I hope my absence hasn't created undo hardship in the office."

"Nah, but it'll be good to have you back."

"It won't be long now, I promise. I'll keep you posted."

Dr. Nutting chuckled. "I guess I just wanted to hear your voice and hear you say that. Now, I'm feeling much better."

"Me, too," Molly said with a smile and tears on her cheeks. "Thanks for calling. I'll be in touch."

Once the cell was flipped closed, Molly wiped her face, dashed to the laundry room, grabbed her tray of cleaning supplies and headed to Worth's room. Usually, Kathy maintained his space, but since Kathy was off ill and had been since the barbecue, Molly felt she had no choice but to tackle it herself.

Besides, it was a wreck. She'd passed his room earlier, paused and took a quick look inside, having no idea what possessed her to do such a thing. Maybe it was because Worth's bed was a mess, like he'd wrestled with a bear and lost.

Whatever, the room needed attention, and she was the only one available. With her Sony Walkman attached to her jeans and her earplugs in, she cleaned his bedroom proper, then moved to the bathroom.

After everything was shining there, with the exception of the shower, she stepped into it and began scrubbing. Although she didn't get wet, she came close to it, her T-shirt anyway. It got damp and, therefore, clung to her breasts like a second skin.

After finishing that job, she removed her ear plugs just in

time to hear a sound, a sound she couldn't identify, though she panicked. Surely it wasn't Worth having come back in. She was positive she'd be in and out of his room before that happened.

Brightening, she told herself she was just hearing things. Still, Molly didn't see any reason to tarry any longer. That was when she opened the door and stepped out, only to freeze in horror.

"You."

She wasn't sure if she spoke the word out loud or not, so shocked was she to see him naked as the day he was born, standing in front of her, staring at her with fire leaping from his widened eyes.

For a moment, they both just stared, him at her breasts with their rosebud nipples thrusting forward and her at his huge, beautiful, growing erection.

"Molly," he said in a voice that sounded like he'd been gutted, then he reached for her.

But she was too fast for him. Before he realized what was happening, she turned and ran out of the room.

"Molly!"

She ignored the plaintive cry she heard in his voice and kept on running. *Out of harm's way.*

Fifteen

Out of sight; out of mind.

She wished.

Worth had been gone for three days, and the thought of seeing him when he returned gave Molly the weak trembles. Realistically, there was no way to avoid the inevitable, and she knew it. He'd at least told Maxine he was going to Dallas to look at some horses. She hadn't expected him to tell her, of course, nor was she complaining. The less she had to do with Worth, the better.

Still, she found herself jumping when she heard a door open or close, which was ludicrous. On this ranch, someone was coming or going all the time.

But she knew from past experience she would look up, turn a corner or walk into a room and there he'd be.

In the glory of his magnificent manhood.

Only clothed, she prayed.

Whenever she thought about that encounter in his bath, she almost lost it. Her breathing turned labored, her limbs trembled and her mind spun.

None of which was good. Or sane.

In fact, since that incident she'd been a basket case. Oh, she'd done what she was supposed to do, probably to perfection because she was so determined to concentrate. She'd taken care of the house, her son and her mother. Yet she'd felt as if it were someone else doing those things—as if she existed outside herself.

Right now Molly found herself pausing and leaning against the cabinet for support, feeling slightly dizzy. Stress. That was all it was. She was under so much pressure that she felt her insides might explode at any second, which was horribly unfair to her son and to her mother.

She had let Worth get under her skin. *Again.*

The sight of him naked had made her crazy with an aching need that wouldn't go away. Although she knew it was wrong to want him to make love to her, she couldn't control her mind. It seemed to have taken on a life of its own.

She didn't know what to do; that was the problem. The more she was around the ranch, the more under Worth's spell she fell. She couldn't leave. Not yet. But soon.

Meanwhile, she would continue to remind herself what Worth had done to her, how he had ripped her heart out and trampled on it. Now that she had Trent, she couldn't dare let that happen again. Even though he had denied it, she felt sure he would eventually marry Olivia. And she was yearning to make love to him.

What kind of woman had she become?

Since she couldn't bear to answer that question, Molly went back to polishing the piece of silver. She was just about finished when Trent rushed into the room.

"Mommy, Mommy!"

"What, darling?"

"Mr. Worth's back."

Molly's heart took a dive, though she kept her tone even and cool. "That's great, honey."

"He wants to take me riding."

Molly panicked. "Oh, Trent, I don't think that's a good idea."

He scrunched up his face.

"You've never ridden a horse, and Mommy's afraid."

"I'm not," he responded with belligerence. "I'm a big boy. You're always telling me that."

"You are a big boy."

His eyes brightened. "Oh goodie, I can go."

"Whoa, cowboy. I didn't say that."

"Mommy! You're being mean."

"Trent," she responded in a stern tone.

"What's going on?"

If she hadn't had such a tight grip on the piece of silver, she would have dropped it at the sound of Worth's voice. The time she'd been dreading had come. He was back, and as suspected, in full sexual glory, sending little tremors of shock to her chest.

"Mommy says I can't go," Trent said to Worth, his lower lip twice its normal size.

"I—" she began.

"I won't let anything happen to him, Molly."

She didn't want to look at Worth, especially with him standing in front of her, staring at her through eyes that were thankfully unreadable. She just hoped she could do the same thing. She'd rather die than to have him know she'd been thinking about how awesome he'd looked naked.

"Molly."

Feeling like her face had just caught on fire, she drew a ragged breath then forced herself to meet his gaze.

"I said I'd take care of him." While his voice had a gruff edge to it, his eyes didn't. They seemed to have suddenly ignited with heat that told her he wasn't as cool and in control as he appeared, that he, too, was remembering the episode in the shower.

And what could have happened, but didn't.

"I just don't think—" Molly's voice played out under that hot, probing gaze.

"Pease, Mommy," Trent begged.

"Oh, all right. Just don't keep him out long, Worth."

"Your wish is my command."

The old sarcastic Worth was back, but she ignored that and added, "I mean it." She knew she sounded unreasonably controlling, but she didn't care. The thought of the two of them alone was like a knife turning in her heart.

But why punish her child for her sins? She couldn't. Besides, she would be leaving soon, and she wouldn't have to worry about those unexpected twists and turns.

"Yippee!" Trent cried, zipping around and running toward the door.

Before Worth followed, a smile almost broke through his tight lips. "I'd say he's excited."

Molly wanted to respond in kind, but her lips felt glued together.

Worth cocked his head to one side. "By the way, I'm having my parents, Olivia and John Lipscomb over tonight."

"For dinner?" Molly asked in a business tone.

"No. Just for snacks and drinks."

"Consider it taken care of."

Worth deliberately perused her body with that cynical curl to his lips. "I never doubted that." He then tipped his hat. "See ya."

Molly attacked the next piece of silver with such vengeance, she almost broke her hand.

* * *

He'd had a great time with the kid, which was both good and bad. The good was that Trent made him laugh, something that he rarely did anymore. It seemed like the laughter had left his body at the same time Molly had left his life.

That kind of thinking was as crazy as it was untrue. Still, more often than not, he realized he walked around with a surly look on his face.

The bad was that the boy made Worth yearn for a son of his own, a gift that would never be his.

Muttering a sailor's curse under his breath, Worth strode into his room where he shed his clothes. It was much later than he'd thought; hence his parents, et al. would soon be arriving. He prided himself on punctuality; this evening was no exception, even if he dreaded what lay ahead.

Lately, his parents got on his nerves big time. Olivia, too. John Lipscomb, his potential campaign manager, was the only one he looked forward to seeing. Suddenly, Worth felt the need for a beer. Maybe that would put him in a better frame of mind.

But since he was naked, he could forget that. *Naked.* He groaned, that word bringing back memories of that bathroom debacle. He laughed without mirth. Who was he kidding? That memory had never left him; since it had happened, it had haunted him day and night.

Even this afternoon, when he'd seen Molly in the kitchen, polishing silver, he could barely remember what she had on, though he figured it was her usual work attire—a pair of low-cut jeans, belt and tight-fitting white shirt.

In his mind, *she* was naked.

Envisioning her perfect breasts, perfect tush, perfect legs, perfect skin and perfect lush lips had shot his libido into over-drive at the same time his control took a kamikaze dive. His body so burned to take her, he'd barely been able to contain himself.

Worth licked his dry lips, wanting a beer more by the second. Again, he glanced at his watch and noticed he scarcely had time to get a shower and dress before the guests arrived. But this was his house, and if he was late, then so be it.

He *needed* a drink.

With that, he slipped back into his jeans and made his way into the kitchen where he pulled up short. Molly was still there—working.

"What the hell?" he said in a rougher tone than he meant.

"Good evening to you, too."

Though he heard the sting in her voice, she kept her gaze averted. He wondered if that was on purpose since she probably saw, out of her peripheral vision, he was only half-dressed.

"Sorry," he muttered, charging for the fridge and grabbing a beer.

"No, you're not." With her head lowered, Molly never stopped arranging fruit on a tray.

He pulled in his breath and stared at a spot where her hair didn't quite touch her collar, thus exposing a bare place on her neck. He clenched his fists, longing to lean over and lick that soft skin, knowing it would feel like velvet under his tongue.

Then realizing what she'd said, he made a face. "What does that mean?"

"You might say you're sorry, but you're not, especially when it pertains to me."

He was about to open his mouth and tell her that was a damned lie. But then he slammed it back shut, knowing she was right. He wasn't sorry he'd spoken harshly to her. Any contact with her now seemed to bring out the worst in him.

Worth wanted what he couldn't have, and that was her. Every time he saw Molly that fact ate a bigger hole in his gut and made him angry to boot, an anger he took out on her. What a freakin' mess.

"You're right, I'm not sorry."

"What do you want?" she asked in a tired voice.

"A beer, which I got." He paused, then added, "You look ready to drop in your tracks."

"I'm about finished."

"Good Lord, Molly, we're not feeding five thousand tonight."

"I haven't fixed for five thousand, either." Her tone was hostile.

His gaze perused the table full of food. "Sure appears that way to me."

She merely looked at him.

Worth shrugged his shoulders. "Okay, so I don't know a damn thing when it comes to entertaining."

"Enough said," Molly responded with a wry tone.

He took another swig of beer before he asked, "Is Kathy helping you serve?"

"No, she's not feeling well."

"Dammit, Molly, you're not superwoman."

Her head popped back. "Who told you that?"

She sounded so serious that for a second, he was so taken aback, he actually laughed.

It was then his eyes trapped hers and the room seemed to tilt. In one giant step Worth ate up the distance between them and was about to reach for her when she skirted around him and dashed for the door.

He muttered an oath.

At the door, she turned but couldn't seem to say anything, which told him she was as shaken as he, especially since her chest was heaving.

Finally, though, in a surprisingly neutral tone, she said, "Thanks for taking Trent riding. He had a great time."

Worth bowed, then responded in his most cynical tone, "My pleasure."

"Dammit, boy, you beat all."

"Now, Dad, if you don't calm down, you're going to have a heart attack."

"No, he isn't," Eva said. "He doesn't have a bad heart. But he might, if you don't stop playing cat and mouse with your future."

"Your mother's right, Worth," John pitched in, his features and voice filled with undisguised concern. "Push has come to shove. You have to make a decision."

His guests had just arrived, and he was already eager for them to go home. The moment after they were seated in the living room and ordered their drinks, they had done nothing but rap on his ears about whether he was going to run for office or not.

The bad part about it was they were right. If he was indeed going to enter the race, he needed to make up his mind and make it up now. But there was just something inside him that kept him from saying the word *yes* and meaning it definitively.

Which probably meant he didn't have the heart of a politician.

"I'm with them, Worth," Olivia said, sidling up closer to him on the sofa, and grabbing his hand, then bringing it up to her lips. For some reason, his gaze went straight to Molly, who was at the bar mixing John a drink. If she saw Olivia's intimate gesture, she chose to ignore it.

No matter. Worth removed his hand with as much grace as possible, suddenly repulsed by Olivia's touch. God, everything that he'd once held near and dear seemed to have gone down the tubes.

Once Molly had handed John his drink, she said, "Is there anything else I can get you?" She paused and smiled. "As you can see, the table is filled with hors d'oeuvres and plenty of sweets."

"Thank you, Molly," Eva said in a stilted tone. "You've done a great job."

Worth knew Molly well enough to sense she was having difficulty keeping a straight face. He also knew that Molly thought his mother was a snob in the truest meaning of the word.

It was in that moment that his and Molly's eyes accidentally met. Later, he told himself he was nuts, but at the time he could've sworn she had winked at him, as though she knew he'd read her mind.

Then Molly smiled again and said, "I'll be back shortly to check on you."

"That won't be necessary," Eva said, turning to Worth. "We won't need her anymore, as we have private matters to discuss. Right, son?"

Worth gave his mother a withering look as he opened his mouth to refute her words. He never got the chance to speak.

Molly beat him to the draw. "Fine, Eva. I'm sure they can depend on you to mix and serve their drinks."

With a horrified look on her face, Eva opened her mouth to speak only nothing came out.

That was when Molly smiled her sweetest smile yet and spoke in her syrupiest southern drawl, "Good night y'all. I sure hope you have a pleasant evening."

Sixteen

Man, he was glad that ordeal was over.

Then Worth felt his conscience pinch him. Those were his folks he was thinking ill of, and the woman he'd been squiring around. Even though he had no intention of marrying her, he should still treat her with respect. As for John, there was no problem. He was a good friend and seemed to want only what was best for Worth.

The others—well, Worth wasn't so sure. That was why his feet were heavy as he made his way toward his bedroom. He paused in his thoughts, toying with the idea of grabbing another beer. Since he'd already had more than his share, he kept going.

His parents and Olivia had tried to pin him to the wall the entire evening, but he'd held firm in his convictions. He still hadn't made up his mind about running for office, which was not like him. *Waffling* was another word that normally wasn't in his vocabulary. Again, until he was fully committed and excited himself, he wasn't going to sign on just to please others.

While the political pressure hadn't been comfortable, it hadn't bothered him nearly as much as his mother's put-down of Molly. When Eva had all but dismissed her as nothing more than a servant, Worth had been furious. Yet he'd kept his mouth shut, which made him despise himself. But what could he have said that wouldn't have sent up a smoke signal? And for what purpose?

He wanted Molly, wanted her so badly he could taste it. But his bodily needs and cravings were nobody's business but his. Besides, nothing would ever come of his hot, scorching desires.

He'd already suffered third-degree burns at her expense, and he didn't have that much skin left to spare. Besides that, she was no longer a road he wanted to travel.

He was certain Molly didn't want to relive that pain and heartache, either. Yet if she didn't hurry up and leave, he wasn't sure he could keep his hands to himself. God, he ached to touch her, to taste her, to…

"Stuff it, Cavanaugh," he muttered, upping his pace down the hall. He was one tired mother and the sooner he got to bed, the sooner his mind would find relief.

He almost laughed at that thought. Since Molly had entered the door of the ranch house, sleep had escaped him, except for short catnaps. Thank goodness, he was lucky he didn't need much shut-eye to keep going.

It was when he passed Molly's room that he heard a sound, a sound he couldn't identify. Not at first, anyway. He paused outside her door and listened.

Sobs.

Muffled.

But gut-wrenching sobs, nonetheless.

Worth continued to stand as though cemented to the spot,

not knowing what to do. Then, as if his hand had a mind of
its own, he slowly twisted the doorknob.

She hated them all, especially Eva.

Molly had never been vindictive and didn't think of herself
as that now. But she'd had enough of those people and could
not wait to get out of their sight, determined never to see
them again.

When she'd been dismissed like a piece of garbage by that
conniving, mean-spirited mother of Worth's, she'd almost
packed her bags, put her son in the car and hauled it out of there.

By the time she returned to her room, took a hot shower,
slipped on a silk nightgown and crawled into bed, she had
calmed down. But not much. Now, as she lay in a fetal
position, resentment and anger welled up inside her, so much
that she wanted to scream. Instead she cried.

Molly didn't know what she'd expected after the attack in
the living room. Yes, she did. She had expected Worth to
defend her, to take up for her. Then she realized that was not
only crazy, but it wasn't going to happen.

After all, he was the leader of the pack against her. From
the get-go, he'd resented the hell out of her—first, for returning to the ranch and second, for staying. The only reason he
tolerated her was because of her mother's health problem.

Another sob stuck in her throat as she curled tighter. If only
she didn't care what Worth thought or did. If only she didn't
care he hadn't come to her rescue verbally.

But she did care, and that was what was killing her.

Trapped.

She felt like a trapped animal, and that didn't sit well with
her. The Cavanaugh clan had already wreaked more havoc in
her life than anyone or anything ever had. And they were
continuing to do so, which made her feel badly about herself.

Especially since she still wanted the one man she could never have. Worth, she had decided, was in her bloodstream, and she would never get rid of him. No matter where she was, if he came around, she would want him. She had decided that would never change. But that didn't mean she had to give in to that desire, that craving of her body.

Once she left the ranch, she would lick her wounds. Time would take care of much of her pain. Too, she had Trent. From the day he was born, he had been the main focus in her life. Once they arrived at the ranch, Worth had cluttered her mind. Once they were back in Houston, Trent would take top priority again.

Her son and her job.

An awesome combination. With both, she could be happy and content once again. She didn't need a man, certainly not one who didn't want her or he wouldn't have let his parents send her away.

She just had to keep Trent and the secret she bore up front in her mind, and she would prevail. Those two things gave her the courage to uncoil her body and try to get some sleep.

Molly had just tossed the blanket back, the gas logs burning low, making cover a bit much, when she heard what sounded like the knob on her door turning. She stilled herself and held her breath.

"Molly?"

Worth!

Oh, God, what should she do?

"Are you all right?"

She could barely hear him as he was as close to whispering as his deep voice would allow.

Pushing the panic button, she remained silent, hoping he'd get the message she didn't want to be disturbed, especially by *him*.

Her ploy failed.

Then the door opened more, and he walked into the shadowy room. Her heart jumped into the back of her throat making speech impossible. Once again her silence backfired, seeming to give him courage to forge forward until he reached the side of her bed.

Molly squeezed her eyes tightly together, praying he would think she'd fallen asleep. She realized, however, that the fresh tears saturating her cheeks said otherwise. When she felt the mattress give beside her, her eyes flew open.

"Worth," she said in an aching tone.

"Shh, it's okay." His voice literally shook with emotion as he stared down at her in the glow of the fire.

"No, it's not," she whimpered, feeling a new set of tears cloud her vision.

"You're right, it's not," he acknowledged in that same emotional voice. "I should've kicked some ass tonight, mine included."

"I want to go home." Her tone was so low, she wasn't sure he had heard her. He had.

"I don't blame you," he said, letting out a shuddering breath.

Another silence.

"You…you should go," Molly whispered, starting to curl into that fetal position again.

"No."

The edge in his voice stopped her cold.

"I want to look at you." His voice now shook. "You're even lovelier than I remembered."

Without thinking, Molly lowered her gaze and saw that her breasts and nipples were swollen and pushing against the silk. When she raised her eyes, fire burned in his, especially when he reached out and removed one strap, exposing one full breast.

His breathing faltered, and he closed his eyes for a moment.

If only she hadn't let Trent spend the night in Maxine's room, she'd have a valid excuse for calling a halt to this madness.

"Molly...please don't send me away."

"Worth, you're not playing fair." She felt desperate not to give in to his pleading, but she felt herself weakening.

"Tell me you don't want me, and I'll go."

"I don't want you."

Worth focused on her with piercing intensity. "Do you really mean that?"

"No...I mean..." She couldn't go on, not when his hand cupped that exposed breast and a moan of despair escaped her.

"God, Molly," he ground out, leaning over and tonguing that bare flesh until the nipple was ripe and pulsating. "I can't leave you now."

In that moment, she was lost. It was beyond her capacity to do anything more than lay there and let him have his way with her. After all, that was what she'd been wanting since the day she'd arrived and had seen him.

Like she'd admitted, he was in her blood and she would never cease to want him. Now was her chance to love him one last time. And she wasn't going to pass it up—right or wrong.

Molly trembled all over when he lifted his face and their eyes clung. Sensing she was his for the taking, Worth cradled her face between his palms and tilted her head toward him. "I need you so much," he said in a low, shaky voice.

She believed him because she felt the same hot need blazing inside her. That summer with him had been the happiest of her life and it had given her the gift of a lifetime— her son. Despite knowing what she knew now, and what she'd been through these past few weeks, she would let him make love to her, even if it put her soul in jeopardy.

He bent to kiss her, and her lips parted to the wet thrust of his tongue as it plunged deeply into her moist cavity. She clutched at him while his hands wandered over her body. It was after she felt a slight chill that she realized he had removed her gown, leaving her naked before him.

Without taking his eyes off her, he stood and removed his clothes, giving her the exquisite luxury of perusing his nakedness. So as to make room for him on the bed, Molly scooted over, and he lay beside her, drawing her to him—flesh against flesh.

His hands circled her back, drawing her close against him, the surge of his manhood waging war against her lower stomach. "You are still the loveliest creature on earth," he told her huskily before his mouth returned to hers with feverish urgency.

She rejoiced in the feel of his lips tangling with hers, especially after he sucked on her tongue, further deepening and lengthening the kiss. Only after they couldn't breathe any longer did he come up for air.

His eyes were glazed with passion, he reached for her leg and swung it over his hip, giving him access to her most sensitive place that he instantly covered with the palm of his hand, then inserted a finger into its warmth.

"Ohh," Molly cried, bouncing her buttocks up. It had been so long since she'd felt this emotion, this high, that only his touch could bring her. Not only did she want his fingers to work their magic, she wanted him inside her, pounding her until she was spent.

And satisfied.

Realizing she was ready for him, she heard his breathing quicken at the same time the burgeoning thickness of his erection tangled in the curls at the entrance to her moist core.

Then it hit her that neither were protected. She drew back.

"Molly?" he asked in a guttural tone. "Please…"

"We…you don't have any protection."

"It's okay," he ground out. "I promise."

"If you say so," she responded in a frantic tone, revealing

how much she wanted him whether he spoke the truth or not. Besides, getting pregnant twice, accidentally, with the same man, was not about to happen, whether it was the right time of the month or not. Fate had to be on her side this time.

She didn't want to think about that now. She only wanted to think about how it would feel to have his hard flesh invade her softness. With only that in mind, Molly reached down, clutched his erection and guided its big, velvet-smooth tip into her aching flesh.

"Oh, my, Molly," he groaned, shoving himself into the heart of her.

She couldn't help but gasp, having forgotten how big he was. Still, her muscles contracted around him; and because she was so ecstatic he was inside her, she framed his face with her hands, bringing his eager lips to hers, where they clung.

She had thought this one last invasion into her flesh would be enough to last her for the rest of her life. She knew better now. When he began to move, and his breathing grew hoarse and labored, she realized she wanted more.

She wanted him forever.

Because that couldn't be, when she felt him empty in her, and she climaxed like never before, she buried her face against his chest so tightly it took her breath.

"Oh, Molly," he cried, shuddering in the aftermath of that awesome coupling. "My Molly."

After it was over, he kissed her all over her face. With him still inside her, he brushed her lips with his, then they both closed their eyes.

And slept.

Seventeen

Molly awoke with a start, especially when she felt her leg entwined with a hard, hairy one. Outwardly, she remained immobile, but inside her was a mass of quivering nerves.

Worth.

Had they made hot, torrid love all night? Surely not. Surely it was only the middle of the night, or earlier. That was why he was still with her. She stole a glance at the clock; it told an entirely different story. It was almost six o'clock. Suddenly she felt like a giant hand was squeezing the life out of her heart.

She could be pregnant. *Again.* Although last night, when they had briefly discussed the fact that no protection was in the offing, he had told her not to worry, and she hadn't. That was because she'd been in the throes of passion and nothing had mattered except feeling Worth inside her.

But with the dawn came reality and with reality came fear.

Yet she didn't want to think about those emotions, especially with Worth's warm body still wrapped around her like a blanket.

Yet she had no choice.

"Worth," she whispered, nudging him awake.

His eyes popped open, and she realized that for a second he, too, was disoriented. Then it apparently hit him where he was; the muted groan against her neck told her that.

"No," she said in a desperate tone.

He paid her no mind, continuing to nuzzle and lick.

Oh, dear Lord, Molly thought, feeling her body weaken then ache for him to make love to her again. But she couldn't allow that, not with Trent having jumped to the forefront of her mind.

"Stop it," she whispered again, this time with more force.

Worth pulled back, confusion mirrored in his eyes. "What's wrong?"

"It's nearly six."

"In the morning?"

"Yes."

"So?" he muttered, still making no effort to dislodge himself.

"You have to go."

"Why? It's my house." Propping himself on his elbow, Worth leaned over and gave her a raw, devouring kiss.

When he pulled his lips off hers, she was as breathless and rattled as she'd ever been. Damn him. He refused to play fair, having stirred her body back to life.

"I loved making love to you," he said in a lazy tone.

Her gaze was intense. "Me, too."

"It was even better than I remembered."

His eyes had turned into banked down coals of fire as she felt him harden against her leg. Somehow she had to get him out of this room, but first she had to know what he'd meant last night when he'd promised she wouldn't get pregnant.

"Worth?"

"Mmm?"

He sounded like his mind was a million miles away, only it wasn't. It was on getting himself inside her again, as he was busy urging her legs apart.

"Why are you so sure I couldn't get pregnant?"

His body went stiff as a plank, and for the longest time he didn't say anything. Then he got back up on his elbow and stared into her face, his features contorted. "Not long after you left I had an accident."

A feeling of dread spread through her. But she didn't say anything. It was up to him to tell her what he wanted her to know, not that it would make any difference, she assured herself. They were destined to live separate lives.

"A horse kicked me in the groin. Kicked the hell out of me, actually."

She winced. "I'm so sorry." And she was. Even though he had hurt her to the core, she didn't wish him any ill will, not when it came to his health.

"Me, too," he said, his tone bleak. "As a result, I probably can't father a child."

Molly almost freaked out, which made speaking, or anything else, impossible.

Only you do have a child, a precious son named Trent.

For the first time since the birth of their son, she yearned to share that news with Worth, to take away the pain she heard in his voice and read in his face.

Only she couldn't.

For her own self-preservation that was impossible, especially with his parents in the picture. However much they might despise her, if they *knew* she had their grandson, they would pull out all the stops to take him away from her. And they had the money and the power to do just that.

As for Worth, she had no idea how that would affect him. She suspected he would follow their lead. Hence, she had no choice but to keep her mouth shut and guard her secret more now than ever.

Which meant she needed to leave ASAP. Today wouldn't be too soon. Knowing that wasn't going to happen, she would be forced to sharpen her acting skills.

She refused to give up Trent or share him with the man who had broken her heart, who was well on his to way to doing it again.

Fool!

"Molly?" he asked in a sandpaper-like tone, placing his lips against her forehead.

"I'm not asleep, if that's what you're thinking."

"Now you know why we can make love all we want to and don't have to worry about it."

She stared at him wide-eyed. "That's where you're wrong."

It was obvious he picked up on the censure in her tone as he pulled his head back, not bothering to mask his confusion.

"This was our swan song, Worth," she said with emphasis.

His jaw went rigid with fury. "So this was our goodbye nookie, huh?"

She knew that crude statement stemmed from the fury that rearranged his features. But she was furious, too, scooting away from him. "Please go," she said in a terse tone.

He reached for her. "Molly, I didn't mean that."

"It doesn't matter," she replied in a dull voice. "This was a mistake and we both know it."

He sighed, but didn't argue, which cut her deeply again. It was then she wondered again how she could have ended up in such a position. But when it came to Worth, she had never used good judgment, and time and years apparently hadn't changed that. But it didn't sit well with her or make her proud of herself. On the contrary, it made her sick to her stomach.

Suddenly thoughts of Trent popped back into her mind.

He was usually a late sleeper. But since he was with her mother, she couldn't make that call. If he were to simply wander back into their suite...

The repercussions of what would happen if he chose to do that this morning didn't bear thinking about. As far as she knew the door was not locked.

Great.

"Worth."

"I'm going, Molly. You've made it quite plain how you feel."

The bitterness was so thick in his voice that for a second she felt sorry for him. Then she mentally kicked her backside for that thought. If it hadn't been for him and his betrayal of her years ago, both their lives would've been different.

Now it was too late.

She would soon go her way and he his.

Jerked back to the moment at hand by him rolling out of bed, Molly found herself gawking at his backside, mainly his buttocks, which were firm and perfect—buttocks she had caressed at will.

When he swung around and stared down at her, she swallowed a labored gasp. Pain was evident in his eyes and face. Only she wasn't looking at his features, God help her. Molly's eyes feasted on the rest of his body, equally as perfect—the muscled arms and chest, the dark hairs—just the right amount— that covered his stomach, down to his fully aroused manhood.

Hot adrenaline rushed through Molly as that turgid flesh made her ache to reach out, and not only caress its big, smooth tip, but surround it with her mouth.

"God, Molly," he whispered in an agonized voice. "If you don't—"

Feeling a flush steal over her face, she quickly averted her gaze and said, "Please leave."

He didn't move immediately; he was too busy uttering harsh obscenities. Then moments passed, and she finally heard the door open and close. Only then did she grab the pillow, hug it close to her chest and let it absorb the tears that freely flowed.

Recriminations?

That soul-searching time had come. Surprisingly, though, she had no regrets. She refused to beat up on herself for letting her body overrule her mind, since she knew it would never happen again.

And for that she was as sad now as she had been the day five years ago she had walked out of his life.

Worth rode the horse until both were tuckered out. Although he hadn't covered anywhere near all of his property, he had achieved his goal.

Riding had definitely tempered the anger that threatened to blow his insides to smithereens. Before Molly had come back to the ranch, he'd been at a crossroads in his life, trying to decide whether he wanted to be a full-time horse breeder or a full-time politician.

Now he was more mixed up and uncertain than ever before. He still wanted to breed horses, but without Olivia's land it wouldn't be on the scale he'd envisioned. And he wanted to run for office, though the fire in his belly still wasn't there.

He was in one big mess.

He blamed Molly. From the moment she had walked in the door of his ranch house, she had screwed with his mind. After yesterday, it was more than his mind. She had screwed with his body. She'd screwed *him*. Not true, he told himself. What they had done had been more than simply screwing. They had made love in the truest sense of the word.

As a result, Worth didn't know how in the hell he was going to keep his hands to himself now that he had gotten another taste of Molly's sweet, succulent flesh.

What awesome, heady stuff. Not only had his body exploded, but his mind, as well. And he wanted more, dammit. But she had made it clear that wasn't going to happen.

Soon she would be gone. That thought made him nudge the horse in the side and send him galloping once again. However, nothing worked to remove the thought, the smell, the feel of Molly from his mind. It was as if she'd been permanently implanted there.

If that were truly the case, then he was in big trouble. This time she would leave and never return. So what could he do about it? Ask her to stay, a little voice whispered, which would be the height of insanity. He couldn't trust her. Hell, she'd run off once. What was to keep her from doing the same thing again?

Nothing.

That was why he couldn't take a chance on exposing his heart and having it broken all over again. Ergo, he had to let her go. And get on with his life.

Some things he could change and some things he could not. Molly happened to fit in the *could not* category.

"Trent," Molly called from the porch, "it's time to wash up for dinner."

Her son didn't answer right off as he was playing with a ball, pretending he was one of the Harlem Globetrotters, and seemed to be having the time of his life. Since it was near dusk, she didn't like him outside alone, and Tammy had already gone home.

"Aw, Mommy, I wanna play a little longer."

"Trent."

"I'll watch him."

As always the sound of Worth's unexpected voice never failed to slam-dunk her nervous system. Dammit, she wished he'd stop appearing out of nowhere.

"Oh, boy, Mommy! Can I stay with Worth?"

She wanted to yell no, but she didn't. Again, why punish her child for her misdeeds? What difference would it make anyway? Their time was on the downhill slide, as her mother was getting better, and stronger, every day.

Their departure couldn't come soon enough because she was beginning to take a trip down Guilt Lane, to beat up on herself, something she had promised she wouldn't do. But Trent needed a father and she knew it.

All boys need a father.

Trent had one he would never know. Suddenly, that thought was overwhelmingly depressing, thinking how much Trent loved this ranch. Not only was she robbing him of his inheritance, she was depriving him of his father.

But if she told the truth, *she* would lose her son.

That couldn't happen.

"Mommy!"

"All right, Trent. You can tag after Worth until supper's ready."

With that she turned and went back into the house, hoping that decision wouldn't come back to haunt her.

Thirty minutes later, Molly returned to the porch and only caught a glimpse of Worth. A frisson of uneasiness ran down her spine. "Worth," she called.

He stopped in his tracks and swung around.

"Where's Trent?"

He made his way closer to her, his features pinched. "I don't know."

"What do you mean you don't know?" Her voice had reached the shrill level.

"Hold on. I'm sure he's okay. I turned my back for a second, and he was gone."

Molly leapt off the porch and ran to Worth. "Where have you looked?" she demanded, trying to keep her panic at bay.

"Everywhere but the barn. That's where I'm headed now."

"Trent!" Molly yelled over and over. No answer.

By the time they reached their destination, Molly was beside herself; her mind had become her own worst enemy. And Worth. She could have gladly strangled him, but since that wasn't possible, she kept her mouth shut, almost choking on her suppressed fury.

"I'm sorry, Molly," he said, entering the shadows of the barn.

She merely flung him a go-to-hell look.

He blanched, but didn't say anything back.

"Trent, are you here?"

"Mommy, Worth, look."

Both pair of eyes shot up to the hayloft. Trent was standing near the edge of the loft that overlooked the cement below. Fear, like poison, spread through her as she stared at Worth. He, too, looked green around the gills, though when he spoke his voice was even and cool.

"Stay where you are, Trent. Don't move."

"Wanna watch me walk—"

"No!" Molly and Worth cried in unison.

The boy froze.

"I'm coming up to get you," Worth said. "Meanwhile, stay right where you are, okay?"

"No, I'll come down."

"Trent, no!"

The boy paid no heed. He turned, then slipped, miraculously falling straight into Worth's outstretched arms.

For a moment no one said a word. It was as though they were all paralyzed. Finally, Trent rallied and said, "Are you mad at me, Mommy?"

"Put him down, Worth," she said with a quiver in her voice.

Worth did as he was told.

Pointing at her son, Molly added, "You go straight to your room and wash up. I'll be there shortly."

Trent hung his head. "Yes, ma'am."

"Go. I'll be watching until you get inside."

As if glad to be away from his mother's wrath for a few minutes at least, Trent took off in a dead run.

Once he disappeared into the house, a heavy silence fell over the barn.

Worth was the first to break it. "You're pissed, and I don't blame you."

"Pissed is too mild for what I am." Her voice dripped with icicles.

"He's okay, Molly. Besides, he's a kid, a boy. They try daring things like that."

"Don't you dare tell me about kids. Especially mine."

"Well, excuse me." His hands clenched. "I told you I was sorry. What more do you want?"

"I don't want anything. Your behavior just proves that your word is as worthless now as it was when you asked me to marry you five years ago."

"What the hell are you talking about?"

"I think we're past the pretend stage, don't you?"

"If you have something to say, then spit it out, 'cause I still don't know what the hell you're talking about."

"Your parents."

"What about my parents?"

"Are you saying you didn't send them to me to try and buy me off?"

Worth rocked back on his heels as though she'd sucker punched him in the gut. "I didn't send them anywhere, and certainly not to talk to you."

"You told me you loved me and wanted to marry me, only to then back out."

"I did no such thing. You're the one who lost your nerve and ran off like a scalded dog."

"Only because of your parents. After they came to me and expressed your feelings, telling me that you didn't love me, but didn't want to tell me for fear of hurting me worse."

Worth's expression turned dark as a thunder cloud.

"Oh, and to further insult me," Molly drilled, "your parents offered me money, lots of money, to get lost."

"That's a lie. You're making all this up to appease your conscience. My parents wouldn't do such a thing."

"Are you calling me a liar?" Molly retorted hotly.

"For God's sake, Molly—"

"Ask them." Her gaze, filled with disdain, wandered over him. "If you've got the guts, that is."

Eighteen

"Son, what a delight," Ted said, opening the door wide enough for Worth to stride through. "You're just in time. Supper will be ready in a few minutes."

"I don't—" Worth never got the rest of the words out, as his mother came around the corner into the living room, a smile on her face.

"What a nice surprise, darling." Eva gestured toward the plush leather sofa near the gas-burning fireplace. "Have a seat," she added with a wink. "I have a feeling you've come to tell us something that will call for a celebration. What can I get you to drink?"

"Nothing, Mother. Please, just sit down and stop talking."

Eva put a hand to her throat. "Why, that's not a very nice way to talk to your mother."

Worth cut his eyes to his father who no longer had that warm look on his face. In fact, his features appeared rather grim, as if he sensed something was terribly wrong. "You, too, Dad. Sit."

Eva's eyes widened. "What on earth is wrong with you? You're acting so unlike yourself." Her frustration and anger seemed to be gaining speed. "You can't just come in here and order us around. This is our house."

"Mother," Worth hissed, "be quiet."

Eva sounded as though she might strangle trying to get further words out of her mouth. Then Ted glanced at her and shook his head, frowning.

Worth watched his mother toss him a go-to-hell look, but she didn't say anything else, thank God. Though she was his mother, he was as close to choking her as he'd ever been in his life.

That was not good, but his fury factor was off the charts, although he was trying his best to keep his emotions under wraps. After all, Molly could be lying to cover her own skin, but his gut told him that wasn't so. Otherwise, she wouldn't have demanded he face his parents.

Besides, he'd reached the end of his rope, and there was nowhere else to go, or anyone else to rescue him—except himself.

"I guess you're not running for office, son," Ted finally said into the uncomfortable silence.

"The election's not why I'm here."

"Then why are you here," Eva demanded in a cold voice, "especially with that mean attitude?" She grabbed a tissue and dabbed at her eyes.

Worth rolled his. "Spare me, Mother, you're mad not sad."

"Stop talking to me like that, Worth Cavanaugh. I've taught you to have respect for your elders, especially your parents. What on earth have we done to make you look at us like you despise us?"

"Does the word *Molly* give you a clue?"

"What about her, son?" Ted asked in a guarded voice.

"Oh, please," Eva put in with added dramatics. "Do we have to talk about her?"

Worth didn't mince any words. "As a matter of fact we do."

"What then?" Eva demanded in a resigned, but sharp tone.

"Did you two have a conversation with her before she left that summer?"

The room got funeral-home quiet.

"I don't know what you're talking about," Eva finally said in her lofty tone. "We had several conversations with that girl."

Worth's ire rose, but when he spoke he still held onto his cool. "That girl, as you call her, was my fiancée."

"Oh, Worth, for crying out loud." Eva flapped a hand with perfectly manicured nails. "She was just your play toy and we knew it."

Worth clenched his teeth, reminding himself that she was his mother, though at the moment he wished he'd never been born to these two selfish snobs.

He couldn't change that, of course. What he could change was the here and now. *And the future.* No more messing around with his life.

"Did you talk to her?" Worth asked again, his gaze including both of them. "And don't lie to me, either."

Eva whipped her head around to Ted who actually looked like all the blood had drained from his face. Worth watched him nod to his wife.

She in turn, faced Worth, her lips stretched in an unbecoming tight line at the same time her eyes sparked. "Yes, we talked to her."

"What did you tell her?" Worth stood and loomed over them. "The exact words."

"Will you please sit down?" Eva asked, clasping her hands together in her lap. "You look like a panther about to pounce, and frankly, that makes me nervous."

"Mother!"

"All right." She raised her eyes to Worth. "We told her you didn't really love her, and that you didn't want to marry her."

An expletive shot out of Worth's mouth.

Eva's head flared back, and she glared at him. However, she seemed to know better than to reprimand him.

"Go on." Worth could hardly get the words through his lips; they were so stiff and his mouth so dry.

"Well, we told her she wasn't good enough for you, but that you didn't want to tell her yourself, so you asked us to do it."

Another string of expletives followed.

Both Eva and Ted sucked in their breaths and held them, staring at him as though their son had suddenly turned into some kind of monster they didn't recognize.

"We…we thought we were doing what was best for you," Eva said in a tearful voice. "We didn't think she was good enough—"

"Your mother's right," Ted chimed in. "We thought we had your best interest—"

"Shut up! Both of you."

Eva's and Ted's mouths dropped open, but they shut up.

Worth leaned in further and spoke in a low, harsh tone. "I loved Molly and intended to marry her. As a result of what you did, you've cost us five miserable years, and the two of you ought to be horsewhipped."

"My God, Worth," Eva cried. "Listen to what you're saying."

He paid her plaintive cry and words no mind. "But because you're my parents, I hope I can find it in my heart to forgive you. Only not now. I don't want to see either of you, so stay away from me, you hear?"

He turned, strode to the door and slammed it behind him with such force, he figured he shattered the expensive glass.

So what? He'd never felt better in his life. Yet he still had a major task in front of him.

Molly.

Despite the chill in the air, sweat broke out on his forehead and his knees threatened to buckle. He had to find Molly and make things right.

"Mama?"

Maxine smiled and patted Molly's hand. "You haven't called me that in a long time. Usually it means you're upset about something."

Molly pulled at the sheet on her mother's bed and finally looked her in the eye. "It's time I left."

Maxine frowned. "That's fine, honey. I'm so much better. In fact, I was thinking about—"

"No. The deal is this. Only if you let me hire a private nurse will I leave."

"I don't need one. I already have a therapist."

"With me gone, you need both. And Worth needs to hire another temporary housekeeper. You have to tell him that. He'll do it for you."

Maxine blew out a frustrated breath. "I sure reared a stubborn child."

"That you did. Those shots in your back, combined with physical therapy, have done wonders. You've made tremendous progress. It's just a matter of time until you'll be your old self."

"Only I'm not quite there yet, right?" Maxine asked with raised brows.

"Not quite."

"While I can hardly bear the thought of you and Trent leaving, you know I understand. On second thought, maybe I don't."

"I just need to get back to the office."

"I think there's more to it than that," Maxine said, then paused. "It's Worth, isn't it?"

Molly could only nod; her throat was too full to speak.

"If he hurt you again, I'll strangle him myself."

"It's okay. It's just time for Trent and me to leave. You love it here. Worth loves you, and I don't want to mess that up."

"I still say you two should've married."

"Well, it's too late for that now," Molly said bitterly.

"It's never too late for happiness, my dear. If it's pride we're talking about here, then let it go. It can bring down the biggest and strongest."

"Mama."

Maxine held up her hand. "I'll say no more. When you're ready to talk, I'm ready to listen. Nothing you've ever done, or could ever do, is unforgivable in my sight. Remember that. I love you more than life itself."

"Oh, Mama," Molly sobbed, leaning over and holding her mother close. "You're my rock and always have been. Maybe it's time I shared my heart."

Maxine reached up and trapped a tear running down her daughter's cheek. "I'm listening, my sweet."

Holding tightly to her mother's hand, Molly began to talk.

She was all packed and ready to go.

Yet she hadn't called Trent. She hadn't had the heart to do so yet as he and Tammy were somewhere on the grounds, running and playing.

She had just walked out on the porch, searching for fresh air that would hopefully calm her nerves, when she heard a knock on the door. She didn't bother to turn around.

"It's open."

When no one said anything, she made her way back inside.

Worth stood leaning against the door frame. Her stomach did its usual thing, and the saliva in her mouth dried up.

"I know I'm the last person you want to see," Worth exclaimed, his gaze zeroing in on the bags on the floor.

"That's right," she said, feeling goose bumps dance up and down her skin.

"I spoke with my parents."

She merely shrugged.

"You were right."

His face seemed to have sunk so that its bones took on new prominence and his voice had a crack in it. That was when she met his tormented gaze head-on.

It was in that moment that Molly knew she still loved him, that she had never stopped and that she would love him until the day she died.

"I'm so sorry they interfered," Worth said, tilting his head as though to keep it above water. "You've got to believe I had no idea any of that garbage had gone on behind my back."

Suddenly a ray of hope burst through the dead spot in Molly's heart, and she saw the possibility of swallowing her pride, like her mother said, and starting anew. If he were willing, that is.

"But that doesn't excuse what you did, Molly."

In one instant, Worth brutally dashed that ray of hope. "And just what did I do?"

"When you left me, you obviously married the first guy you met and screwed his brains out."

For the longest time Molly couldn't speak. The pain and humiliation were so severe, it put a vise on her throat. Finally, though, she rallied and spat, "How dare you say a thing like that to me? Have you no shame?"

"Tell me it isn't true." Worth's tone remained unrelenting. "And I'll take it back."

"Of course, it's not true."

His features contorted. "Then, dammit, what is the truth?"

Almost choking on her words, Molly lashed back, "I never married. I made up that story for my and Trent's protection."

"Okay, so you never married. You just screwed his brains out!"

"No, I didn't!" Molly cried out in fury.

"Well, you obviously let *someone* have your body," Worth said with a sneer.

Molly felt her fury rise to a new level. How could the man she loved say such awful things to her? She felt her face heat as words came screaming from her mouth. "No man has ever touched me but you!"

God, how could she have said that? She clasped her hands over her mouth to stop a wail from escaping. Molly knew the answer, and it made her sick at heart and sick to her stomach. She had been goaded into revealing the one secret she had sworn to take to her grave. But words, like arrows, once released, could never be recalled. The damage had been done.

Standing stonelike, she watched Worth's face as her words sank in. A myriad of emotions crossed it, none of which she could read. Was he already planning how he was going to rip Trent out of her arms and claim him as his own? With his money and power, Worth certainly had the means and power to do so.

Molly grasped her stomach, giving in to the fear that stampeded through her.

Worth, meanwhile, crossed the room with lighting speed, grabbed her arm and demanded in a raspy voice, "Did you say what I think you said?"

She could only stare at him, searching frantically for the words to right a wrong. She could deny what she'd said, or she could remain mute and let her words speak for themselves.

"God, Molly, please tell me. Is Trent my son?" Worth moaned softly. "But even if he isn't, it doesn't matter. I don't think I can live a moment longer without you."

Without thought, Molly's hands came up, encased his face and delved deeply into his eyes. "We—Trent and I come as a package deal," she murmured around the tears clogging her throat.

"So, he is my son," Worth said, his voice husky with emotion.

"Yes," Molly whispered. "Trent's your son."

He rocked back on his heels, his breath coming in heaves. Molly instinctively reached out a hand. "Worth?"

Worth clasped her hand and said, "Trent's really mine?" This time awe filled his voice and tears filled his eyes.

She pulled back and peered into his contorted features. "Yes, yes, yes."

"Oh, God, Molly, I can't believe that."

"Do you hate me for not telling you?"

He didn't hesitate. "I could never hate you for anything," he said fiercely. "I love you too much. In fact, you're the only woman I've ever loved."

"And you're the only man I've ever loved," she replied breathlessly.

"Molly…" He pulled her into his arms and simply held her for the longest, sweetest time. Then peering down at her, he said, "I want you. I need you. But most of all I love you, and I'll never let you go again."

He kissed her, then, so hard, so long, and so deep and held her so tightly, she couldn't tell whose heartbeat was whose. It didn't matter; in that moment they became one.

One Year Later

"Oh, yes, Molly, don't stop."

"As if I would," she whispered, atop Worth, continuing to ride him, slowly, then faster, until they climaxed simultaneously.

Exhausted, she fell onto his chest, hearing their hearts beat as one.

Moments later, Worth maneuvered so that he could get to her lips, giving her a long, tender kiss. Only he didn't stop there; he lifted her a little more and put those lips to one breast, then the other, and sucked.

"Ohh," Molly whispered. "You're about to get something started again."

Worth chuckled at the same time he rolled her over so that she was now under him. "That's my intention."

"But it's so soon," Molly pointed out with an answering chuckle. "You...we just came."

"I know, but don't you feel him growing, even as I'm speaking?"

Molly merely sighed and placed her arms around him. For the longest time thereafter, the room was quiet except for their moans.

A short time later, they faced each other satisfied, but worn out from their marathon evening of lovemaking.

"So, Mrs. Cavanaugh, how was your day?" Worth asked in a husky tone, his eyes still a bit glazed over with passion.

"Good, Mr. Cavanaugh. How was yours?"

"Busy as hell."

"That's a good thing, right?"

"Right, my precious."

Molly was quiet for a moment, reveling in the glow of happiness that had surrounded them since that day they both learned the truth about their pasts. Although they had yet to tell Trent that Worth was his real father, it didn't matter, at least not now.

When they told him they were in love and were going to get married, Trent had asked if he could call Worth daddy.

Thinking back on that day still tugged at Molly's heart and would be forever imprinted there.

She had cooked a special dinner with all the trimmings—candlelight, flowers, pot roast, Italian cream cake—wine for them, a Shirley Temple for Trent. Once the meal was over, they had gone into the living room where Worth had reached for Trent's hand, drawing the child onto his lap.

"Your mom and I have something to tell you," Worth said in a none-too-steady voice.

"What?" Trent mumbled, eyeing his mother and sounding uncertain.

"It's okay, sweetie," she responded with a smile and a wink.

"How would you like to live here all the time?" Worth asked, also smiling.

"Wow!" Trent cut his gaze back to his mother.

Molly grinned. "That's what I think, too."

"Your mom and I are in love and want to get married."

Trent made a face. "Does that mean you'll be kissing Mommy all the time?"

Both adults laughed without restraint.

"I'm afraid so," Worth finally admitted, having regained his composure.

"I guess that'd be okay." Trent cocked his head to one side as if trying to figure out how best to communicate what was churning in his little mind. "Would you be my daddy?"

"You betcha."

Trent seemed to think on that for a moment during which Molly held her breath. She suspected Worth was doing likewise.

"Can I call you Daddy?"

Worth's mouth worked. "I'd like that a lot."

A smile broke across the child's face. "Man, now I'll be like all my friends. They all have daddies."

Molly looked on as Worth grabbed Trent and hugged him

tightly, all the while seeking her eyes that were filled with tears. Only after blinking them away did she see the ones in Worth's.

Several days later she and Worth exchanged vows. From that moment on, they had become a family.

During the year they had been married, her mother's back had completely mended. And though she had insisted on keeping her job as housekeeper, Worth had said no, that it was time for her to retire and enjoy life—mainly her grandson.

Maxine hadn't argued, and thus was having a ball.

As for Eva and Ted, they were another story altogether. Even though civility became the order of the day, a wedge remained between Worth and his parents. While Molly hated that, and felt responsible to some degree, there was nothing she could do. Worth had to work through his problems with his parents in his own way and in his own time.

Following that fierce altercation with Ted and Eva, Worth had decided not to run for office, vowing, instead, to concentrate on making her and Trent happy, along with building his horse breeding empire. He and Art had figured a way to make it work without Olivia's land.

"You're awfully quiet," Worth said, interrupting her thoughts, dropping a kiss on the tip of her nose.

"I was just thinking about this past year and everything that's happened."

"Such as?"

"Us. Trent. Your estrangement from your family."

Worth grimaced. "I've been thinking about that, too, but right now I still can't get past their mean-spiritedness."

"Maybe one day you can because of Trent. They are, after all, his grandparents, and I want him to know them."

"You're right, of course. I'm sure they're sorry and are suffering, but I can't completely forgive, nor can I forget." His rimace deepened. "They cost me almost five years of my on's life."

"I know how deeply that cuts, but—"

"You think I should try and make amends?"

Molly nodded her head. "I'd like that for the reason I just aid, Trent. However, it's your call as to how you handle our folks."

"Well, Christmas is knocking on the door." He paused. We'll see what that brings."

Molly smiled, then kissed him. "You're a good man, Worth Cavanaugh."

"And you're a liar, Molly Cavanaugh. I'm a son of a bitch nd we both know it."

They giggled, then hugged.

"Do you miss your work?" he asked when their laughter ubsided.

"A little," she said truthfully. "I miss Dr. Nutting, my old oss, but he certainly understands why I didn't return."

"Have you thought about working here full time? I want ou to be happy at home, but if not, that's okay."

She heard the forlorn note in her husband's voice and aughed. "Are you sure about that?"

He grinned. "Well, I might be a tad jealous."

"Actually, I was thinking about doing some volunteer work t the local clinic a couple of days a week. That way I can keep ny license current. I just hadn't gotten around to telling you."

"Hey, that's a great idea."

"I thought so, too." Molly stretched, and in doing so, xposed a nipple to his greedy eyes and lips. He latched on o it and sucked.

"You know our life is pretty much perfect," she whispered, even if I am married to a badass."

He laughed again, then sobered. "I just wish we could have

another child. I'd like to be there for the whole meal deal, so to speak, watching your belly grow and feeling our child move."

"There's no time like the present to get started."

Worth gave her a perplexed look. "You know what the doctor said."

"Doctors don't walk on water. They make mistakes every day. I suggest we begin right now proving yours wrong. And the rest of our tomorrows, if that's what it takes."

"Oh, God, Molly," Worth whispered, tossing a leg over her hip, "I wouldn't want to live life without you."

"Nor I without you." She smiled at him with love. "So how about we get busy and make that baby."

* * * * *

Ambience is everything. Imagine eating a foie gras at a luncheonette counter or a side of coleslaw at Le Cirque. It's not a matter of food but one of atmosphere. Remember that when planning your dining room design.
—Tips from *Teddi.com*

"Now that's the kind of man you should be looking for," my mother, the self-appointed keeper of my shelf-life stamp, says. She points with her fork at a man in the corner of the Steak-Out Restaurant, a dive I've just been hired to redecorate. Making this restaurant look four-star will be hard, but not half as hard as getting through lunch without strangling the woman across the table from me. "*He* would make a good husband."

"Oh, you can tell that from across the room?" I ask, wondering how it is she can forget that when we had trouble getting rid of my last husband, she shot him. "Besides being ten minutes away from death if he actually eats all that steak, he's twenty years too old for me and—shallow woman that I am—twenty pounds too heavy. Besides, I am *so* not looking for another husband here. I'm looking to design a new image for this place, looking for some sense of ambience, some feeling, something I can build a proposal on for them."

My mother studies the man in the corner, tilting her head, the better to gauge his age, I suppose. I think she's grimacing, but with all the Botox and Restylane injected into that face, it's hard to tell. She takes another bite of her steak salad, chews slowly so that I don't miss the fact that the steak is a poor cut and tougher than it should be. "You're concentrating on the wrong kind of proposal," she says finally. "Just look at this place, Teddi. It's a dive. There are hardly any other diners. What does *that* tell you about the food?"

"That they cater to a dinner crowd and it's lunchtime," I tell her.

I don't know what I was thinking bringing her here with me. I suppose I thought it would be better than eating alone. There really are days when my common sense goes on vacation. Clearly, this is one of them. I mean, really, did I not resolve less than three weeks ago that I would not let my mother get to me anymore?

What good are New Year's resolutions, anyway?

Mario approaches the man's table and my mother studies him while they converse. Eventually Mario leaves the table with a huff, after which the diner glances up and meets my mother's gaze. I think she's smiling at him. That or she's got indigestion. They size each other up.

I concentrate on making sketches in my notebook and try to ignore the fact that my mother is flirting. At nearly seventy, she's developed an unhealthy interest in members of the opposite sex to whom she isn't married.

According to my father, who has broken the TMI rule and given me Too Much Information, she has no interest in sex with him. Better, I suppose, to be clued in on what they aren't doing in the bedroom than have to hear what they might be doing.

"He's not so old," my mother says, noticing that I have

barely touched the Chinese chicken salad she warned me not to get. "He's got about as many years on you as you have on your little cop friend."

She does this to make me crazy. I know it, but it works all the same. "Drew Scoones is not my little 'friend.' He's a detective with whom I—"

"Screwed around," my mother says. I must look shocked, because my mother laughs at me and asks if I think she doesn't know the "lingo."

What I thought she didn't know was that Drew and I actually tangled in the sheets. And, since it's possible she's just fishing, I sidestep the issue and tell her that Drew is just a couple of years younger than me and that I don't need reminding. I dig into my salad with renewed vigor, determined to show my mother that Chinese chicken salad in a steak place was not the stupid choice it's proving to be.

After a few more minutes of my picking at the wilted leaves on my plate, the man my mother has me nearly engaged to pays his bill and heads past us toward the back of the restaurant. I watch my mother take in his shoes, his suit and the diamond pinkie ring that seems to be cutting off the circulation in his little finger.

"Such nice hands," she says after the man is out of sight. "Manicured." She and I both stare at my hands. I have two popped acrylics that are being held on at weird angles by bandages. My cuticles are ragged and there's marker decorating my right hand from measuring carelessly when I did a drawing for a customer.

Twenty minutes later she's disappointed that he managed to leave the restaurant without our noticing. He will join the list of the ones I let get away. I will hear about him twenty years from now when—according to my mother—my children will be grown and I will still be single, living pathetically alone with several dogs and cats.

After my ex, that sounds good to me.

The waitress tells us that our meal has been taken care of by the management and, after thanking Mario, the owner, complimenting him on the wonderful meal and assuring him that once I have redecorated his place people will be flocking here in droves (I actually use those words and ignore my mother when she rolls her eyes), my mother and I head for the restroom.

My father—unfortunately not with us today—has the patience of a saint. He got it over the years of living with my mother. She, perhaps as a result, figures he has the patience for both of them, and feels justified having none. For her, no rules apply, and a little thing like a picture of a man on the door to a public restroom is certainly no barrier to using the john. In all fairness, it does seem silly to stand and wait for the ladies' room if no one is using the men's room.

Still, it's the idea that rules don't apply to her, signs don't apply to her, conventions don't apply to her. She knocks on the door to the men's room. When no one answers she gestures to me to go in ahead. I tell her that I can certainly wait for the ladies' room to be free and she shrugs and goes in herself.

Not a minute later there is a bloodcurdling scream from behind the men's room door.

"Mom!" I yell. "Are you all right?"

Mario comes running over, the waitress on his heels. Two customers head our way while my mother continues to scream.

I try the door, but it is locked. I yell for her to open it and she fumbles with the knob. When she finally manages to unlock and open it, she is white behind her two streaks of blush, but she is on her feet and appears shaken but not stirred.

"What happened?" I ask her. So do Mario and the waitress and the few customers who have migrated to the back of the place.

She points toward the bathroom and I go in, thinking it serves her right for using the men's room. But I see nothing amiss.

She gestures toward the stall, and, like any self-respecting and suspicious woman, I poke the door open with one finger, expecting the worst.

What I find is worse than the worst.

The husband my mother picked out for me is sitting on the toilet. His pants are puddled around his ankles, his hands are hanging at his sides. Pinned to his chest is some sort of Health Department certificate.

Oh, and there is a large, round, bloodless bullet hole · between his eyes.

Four Nassau County police officers are securing the area, waiting for the detectives and crime scene personnel to show up. They are trying, though not very hard, to comfort my mother, who in another era would be considered to be suffering from the vapors. Less tactful in the twenty-first century, I'd say she was losing it. That is, if I didn't know her better, know she was milking it for everything it was worth.

My mother loves attention. As it begins to flag, she swoons and claims to feel faint. Despite four No Smoking signs, my mother insists it's all right for her to light up because, after all, she's in shock. Not to mention that signs, as we know, don't apply to her.

When asked not to smoke, she collapses mournfully in a chair and lets her head loll to the side, all without mussing her hair.

Eventually, the detectives show up to find the four patrolmen all circled around her, debating whether to administer

CPR, smelling salts or simply call the paramedics. I, however, know just what will snap her to attention.

"Detective Scoones," I say loudly. My mother parts the sea of cops.

"We have to stop meeting like this," he says lightly to me, but I can feel him checking me over with his eyes, making sure I'm all right while pretending not to care.

"What have you got in those pants?" my mother asks him, coming to her feet and staring at his crotch accusingly. "*Baydar?* Everywhere we Bayers are, you turn up. You don't expect me to buy that this is a coincidence, I hope."

Drew tells my mother that it's nice to see her, too, and asks if it's his fault that her daughter seems to attract disasters.

Charming to be made to feel like the bearer of a plague.

He asks how I am.

"Just peachy," I tell him. "I seem to be making a habit of finding dead bodies, my mother is driving me crazy and the catering hall I booked two freakin' years ago for Dana's bat mitzvah has just been shut down by the Board of Health!"

"Glad to see your luck's finally changing," he says, giving me a quick squeeze around the shoulders before turning his attention to the patrolmen, asking what they've got, whether they've taken any statements, moved anything, all the sort of stuff you see on TV, without any of the drama. That is, if you don't count my mother's threats to faint every few minutes when she senses no one's paying attention to her.

Mario tells his waitstaff to bring everyone espresso, which I decline because I'm wired enough. Drew pulls him aside and a minute later I'm handed a cup of coffee that smells divinely of Kahlúa.

The man knows me well. Too well.

His partner, whom I've met once or twice, says he'll interview the kitchen staff. Drew asks Mario if he minds if he takes statements from the patrons first and gets to him and the wait-staff afterward.

"No, no," Mario tells him. "Do the patrons first." Drew raises his eyebrow at me like he wants to know if I get the double entendre. I try to look bored.

"What it is with you and murder victims?" he asks me when we sit down at a table in the corner.

I search them out so that I can see you again, I almost say, but I'm afraid it will sound desperate instead of sarcastic.

My mother, lighting up and daring him with a look to tell her not to, reminds him that *she* was the one to find the body.

Drew asks what happened *this time*. My mother tells him how the man in the john was "taken" with me, couldn't take his eyes off me and blatantly flirted with both of us. To his credit, Drew doesn't laugh, but his smirk is undeniable to the trained eye. And I've had my eye trained on him for nearly a year now.

"While he was noticing you," he asks me, "did *you* notice anything about him? Was he waiting for anyone? Watching for anything?"

I tell him that he didn't appear to be waiting or watching. That he made no phone calls, was fairly intent on eating and did, indeed, flirt with my mother. This last bit Drew takes with a grain of salt, which was the way it was intended.

"And he had a short conversation with Mario," I tell him. "I think he might have been unhappy with the food, though he didn't send it back."

Drew asks what makes me think he was dissatisfied, and I tell him that the discussion seemed acrimonious and that Mario looked distressed when he left the table. Drew makes a note and says he'll look into it and asks about anyone else in the restaurant. Did I see anyone who didn't seem to belong, anyone who was watching the victim, anyone looking suspicious?

"Besides my mother?" I ask him, and Mom huffs and blows her cigarette smoke in my direction.

I tell him that there were several deliveries, the kitchen staff going in and out the back door to grab a smoke. He stops me and asks what I was doing checking out the back door of the restaurant.

Proudly—because, while he was off forgetting me, dropping by only once in a while to say hi to Jesse, my son, or drop something by for one of my daughters that he thought they might like, I was getting on with my life—I tell him that I'm decorating the place.

He looks genuinely impressed. "Commercial customers? That's great," he says. Okay, that's what he *ought* to say. What he actually says is "Whatever pays the bills."

"Howard Rosen, the famous restaurant critic, got her the job," my mother says. "You met him—the good-looking, distinguished gentleman with the *real* job, something to be proud of. I guess you've never read his reviews in *Newsday*."

Drew, without missing a beat, tells her that Howard's reviews are on the top of his list, as soon as he learns how to read.

"I only meant—" my mother starts, but both of us assure her that we know just what she meant.

"So," Drew says. "Deliveries?"

I tell him that Mario would know better than I, but that I saw vegetables come in, maybe fish and linens.

"This is the second restaurant job Howard's got her," my mother tells Drew.

"At least she's getting *something* out of the relationship," he says.

"If he were here," my mother says, ignoring the insinuation, "he'd be comforting her instead of interrogating her. He'd be making sure we're both all right after such an ordeal."

"I'm sure he would," Drew agrees, then looks me in the eyes as if he's measuring my tolerance for shock. Quietly he adds, "But then maybe he doesn't know just what strong stuff your daughter's made of."

It's the closest thing to a tender moment I can expect from Drew Scoones. My mother breaks the spell. "She gets that from me," she says.

Both Drew and I take a minute, probably to pray that's all I inherited from her.

"I'm just trying to save you some time and effort," my mother tells him. "My money's on Howard."

Drew withers her with a look and mutters something that sounds suspiciously like "fool's gold." Then he excuses himself to go back to work.

I catch his sleeve and ask if it's all right for us to leave. He says sure, he knows where we live. I say goodbye to Mario. I assure him that I will have some sketches for him in a few days, all the while hoping that this murder doesn't cancel his redecorating plans. I need the money desperately, the alternative being borrowing from my parents and being strangled by the strings.

My mother is strangely quiet all the way to her house. She doesn't tell me what a loser Drew Scoones is—despite his good looks—and how I was obviously drooling over him. She doesn't ask me where Howard is taking me tonight or warn me not to tell my father about what happened because he will worry about us both and no doubt insist we see our respective psychiatrists.

She fidgets nervously, opening and closing her purse over and over again.

"You okay?" I ask her. After all, she's just found a dead man on the toilet and tough as she is that's got to be upsetting.

When she doesn't answer me I pull over to the side of the road.

"Mom?" She refuses to meet my eyes. "You want me to take you to see Dr. Cohen?"

She looks out the window as if she's just realized we're on Broadway in Woodmere. "Aren't we near Marvin's Jewelers?" she asks, pulling something out of her purse.

"What have you got, Mother?" I ask, prying open her fingers to find the murdered man's ring.

"It was on the sink," she says in answer to my dropped jaw. "I was going to get his name and address and have you return it to him that he could ask you out. I thought it was a sign that the two of you were meant to be together."

"He's dead, Mom. You understand that, right?" I ask. You never can tell when my mother is fine and when she's in la-la land.

"Well, I didn't know that," she shouts at me. "Not at the time."

I ask why she didn't give it to Drew, realize that she wouldn't give Drew the time in a clock shop and add, "…or one of the other policemen?"

"For heaven's sake," she tells me. "The man is dead, Teddi, and I took his ring. How would that look?"

Before I can tell her it looks just the way it is, she pulls out a cigarette and threatens to light it.

"I mean, really," she says, shaking her head like it's my brains that are loose. "What does he need with it now?"

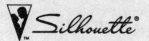

In February, expect **MORE**
from

HARLEQUIN *Romance*

as it increases to six titles per month.

What's to come...

Rancher and Protector

Part of the

Western Weddings
miniseries

BY JUDY CHRISTENBERRY

The Boss's Pregnancy Proposal

BY RAYE MORGAN

Don't miss February's
incredible line up of authors!

REQUEST YOUR FREE BOOKS!

2 FREE NOVELS PLUS 2 FREE GIFTS!

Passionate, Powerful, Provocative!

YES! Please send me 2 FREE Silhouette Desire® novels and my 2 FREE gifts. After receiving them, if I don't wish to receive any more books, I can return the shipping statement marked "cancel." If I don't cancel, I will receive 6 brand-new novels every month and be billed just $3.80 per book in the U.S., or $4.47 per book in Canada, plus 25¢ shipping and handling per book and applicable taxes, if any*. That's a savings of almost 15% off the cover price! I understand that accepting the 2 free books and gifts places me under no obligation to buy anything. I can always return a shipment and cancel at any time. Even if I never buy another book from Silhouette, the two free books and gifts are mine to keep forever.

225 SDN EEXJ   326 SDN EEXU

Name	(PLEASE PRINT)

Address		Apt.

City	State/Prov.	Zip/Postal Code

Signature (if under 18, a parent or guardian must sign)

Mail to Silhouette Reader Service™:

IN U.S.A.
P.O. Box 1867
Buffalo, NY
14240-1867

IN CANADA
P.O. Box 609
Fort Erie, Ontario
L2A 5X3

Not valid to current Silhouette Desire subscribers.

Want to try two free books from another line?
Call 1-800-873-8635 or visit www.morefreebooks.com.

* Terms and prices subject to change without notice. NY residents add applicable sales tax. Canadian residents will be charged applicable provincial taxes and GST. This offer is limited to one order per household. All orders subject to approval. Credit or debit balances in a customer's account(s) may be offset by any other outstanding balance owed by or to the customer. Please allow 4 to 6 weeks for delivery.

SDES06

Silhouette®

SPECIAL EDITION™

Logan's Legacy Revisited

**THE LOGAN FAMILY IS BACK
WITH SIX NEW STORIES.**

Beginning in January 2007 with

THE COUPLE
MOST LIKELY TO

by

LILIAN DARCY

Tragedy drove them apart. Reunited eighteen
years later, their attraction was once again
undeniable. But had time away changed
Jake Logan enough to let him face his fears
and commit to the woman he once loved?

nocturne™

**WAS HE HER SAVIOR
OR HER NIGHTMARE?**

HAUNTED
LISA CHILDS

Years ago, Ariel and her sisters were separated for
their own protection. Now the man who vowed
revenge on her family has resumed the hunt, and
Ariel must warn her sisters before it's too late.
The closer she comes to finding them, the more
secretive her fiancé becomes. Can she trust the man
she plans to spend eternity with? Or has he been
waiting for the perfect moment to destroy her?

On sale December 2006.

Don't miss
DAKOTA FORTUNES,
a six-book continuing series following
the Fortune family of South Dakota—
oil is in their blood and privilege
is their birthright.

This series kicks off with
USA TODAY bestselling author
PEGGY MORELAND'S
Merger of Fortunes
(SD #1771)

this January.